MURDER ON THE ROCKS

Also By Robert Dietrich

The Steve Bentley Series

Murder on the Rocks
End of a Stripper
The House on Q Street
Mistress to Murder
Murder on Her Mind
Angel Eyes
Curtains for a Lover
Steve Bentley's Calypso Caper
My Body
Guilty Knowledge

MURDER ON THE ROCKS

ROBERT DIETRICH

CUTTING EDGE

ISBN-13: 978-1-952138-05-8

Published by
Cutting Edge Publishing
PO Box 8212
Calabasas, CA 91372
www.cuttingedgebooks.com

CHAPTER ONE

If you've been around Washington, you'll know Hogan's, Main Avenue near the Municipal Fish Wharf. Draft beer, Formica table tops, steel cutlery, and the best seafood north of New Orleans. The Negro waiters are faster than Japanese jugglers and most of them have worked at Hogan's since before the war with Spain. The main room has maple paneling, linoleum floor tile, and a few game fish mounted on oak trophy plaques. The coral and dried starfish are for tourists who can't leave town without a meal at Hogan's to tell about at the next Lions' meeting in Sassafras, Missouri. On the side next to the bait shop there is an open doorway with a script neon sign that spells Cocktail Lounge. Inside, there is just enough light to read a drink list in Braille if you have sensitive fingers, and that's for the civil servants who crowd Hogan's every noon in the hot months. White-collar workers from Agriculture and Interior and Labor and the Bureau of Engraving. Men and women with humdrum jobs, enough money to get along on, and a gnawing fear of loneliness.

It was Saturday afternoon. Outside, on the sidewalk, you could broil whole swordfish, but Hogan's air conditioner was a blessed wind. The time was three o'clock. I was finishing an order of Crab Norfolk, and I was on my fourth draft ale. I had worked late to finish a tax case and have the rest of the week-end free. My ketch was tugging at a Yacht Club buoy three blocks away, its icebox jammed with beer and cold cuts, and within the hour I planned to be tacking down the quiet Potomac, a line over the stern. Down past Mount Vernon, anchoring for the night in Gunston Cove.

As the waiter cleared the table and brought apple pie and coffee, I began to relax. I had been working too hard; the end of the fiscal year brought a rush of tax problems, but now the bulk was over and for the rest of July I could slow the pace. My vacation was set for the last two weeks in August, and it looked like a peaceful summer.

At three in the afternoon even Hogan's was peaceful. From the cocktail lounge drifted the occasional tinkle of glasses and the strum of low conversation. I was alone in the restaurant except for a girl at the wall table. As I began to eat my pie I looked at her. Her profile was clean; she had high cheekbones that made little hollows in her cheeks, dark black hair that brushed bare shoulders, and skin that looked carefully tanned. Her fingers toyed with a chilled copper flagon of Pimm's No. 1 Cup and, as I watched, she lifted it to her lips, drained it, and beckoned to the waiter. Then she took a cigarette from her handbag and lighted it. Sitting by herself she looked lonely and thoughtful, absorbed by some private trouble, or perhaps by loneliness itself. I would have written her off as a government secretary except for the dress she was wearing. It was made of Siamese silk, an iridescent blue-green color, and it was an evening dress. In Hogan's eatery, at three o'clock on a Saturday afternoon. And drinking Pimm's No. 1 Cup. The combination was odder than red hair on a Bantu tribesman.

It changed things. It made her someone's doll. That or a nonconformist spirit with money enough to dress and do as she pleased. For a while I juggled the possible combinations, thought the hell with it, and finished my pie. I was fumbling with my money clip when she got up, lifted the copper flagon, and walked toward me. Her stride was measured and graceful—her carriage erect. Not stiff but poised, as though she balanced books on her head every day of her life. Putting the drink on the edge of the table, she smiled and said, "It's awfully hot, don't you think?"

"Outside it is."

"Of course. I didn't mean here. It's very comfortable in here. In fact, almost too cool." Her hand touched her shoulder.

"It's hot because it's Washington. In July. Around Nashville it's even hotter, and they say Tucson this time of year is enough to give anyone the fantods. Of course, south of the Equator the seasons are reversed. In Sydney, for example, it's probably snowing like anything. Could that cover the weather?"

She pulled back a chair, gathered the folds of her skirt, and sat down. She picked up the flagon, tilted it, and drank. Then she lowered it and smiled at me. A slow smile, amused and sultry and a little maddening. She said, "Probably you think I'm a pickup."

"I hadn't thought about it much, but I'll say this: if you're a pickup you're something way out of the ordinary."

"A thousand thanks." She laughed then. An easy silvery laugh that parted white even teeth. Her chin tilted and the oblique angle gave her eyes an almond look. The iris was green, dark green, the eyelashes bigger than butterflies. As I watched, her face seemed to come into focus suddenly and I realized that somewhere, sometime, I had seen her before.

The waiter brought my check and I laid a bill on his tray.

Her face became serious. "You aren't leaving?"

"Tell me why I'm not?"

She shrugged. "Because it's so funny. You don't know me and I know you. Aren't you even intrigued?"

"Let me guess," I said. "Sure, you're Mabel Snodgrass from Rocky Point Junior High. I recollect we used to throw spitballs at each other and all like that. Hi, Mabel."

The waiter brought my change. I let it ride and stood up.

Her eyes followed me. She said, "You're Steve Bentley. I told you I knew who you were."

"That's mighty interesting," I told her. "Where some fellows might blush all over at a quick make like that, it just makes me curious. Mildly."

"And you don't know who I am?"

"Should I?"

She smiled again, stretching her arms lazily. "I'm Iris Sewall. Once I was Iris Calvo. Remember now?"

I remembered. Her father was an Ambassador from somewhere in South America. I remembered endless society page photographs captioned Latin Beauty, and one in particular I'd seen on a Pusan billet wall showing her being crowned Queen of the President's Cup Races. I sat down.

She said, "I suppose I resemble a minor catastrophe today. Last night was a large party over in Warrenton and somehow I never got to bed." She picked up the flagon and drained it. "The best thing seemed to be to keep on drinking."

"It scarcely shows," I said. She looked fresher than a crisp dollar bill.

"How nice. Jean said you could be gracious."

"Jean?"

"Jean MacIntyre. You used to go with her. Only her name wasn't MacIntyre then. It was Ross. Remember?"

"Of course."

She nodded thoughtfully. "We were classmates at Fentriss, Jean and I. Best friends. I wore braces on my teeth then and I was keen on field hockey, so you wouldn't remember me. It was years ago."

She signaled the waiter. I glanced at my watch and said, "Look, I—"

"Don't leave. I had hell's own time finding you. After I made up my mind, that is."

"Miss Calvo," I said, "or Mrs. Sewall, or whatever your name is, I've had a hard spring, a hard month, and so far a hard day. Please don't complicate it by being devious. I shouldn't be here at all. By now I ought to be halfway down Washington Channel with not a care in the world. I'm flattered you took the trouble to get in touch with me, and if it's a tax matter I'll be in my office after nine o'clock Monday morning. Could it keep until then?"

"No," she said abruptly. "It won't keep at all. The fact that I came here to find you ought to indicate some urgency on my part."

"Maybe. Just how did you happen to know I'd even be here?"

"I called your apartment at ten but you weren't there. I didn't think of calling your office until just before noon because nobody works on Saturday in Washington in the summer."

"I do," I said. "Some labor while others play. A thousand worker bees for every drone."

She shrugged. "Your secretary said you'd be here."

I pushed back the chair and stood up. "Uh-uh. Yesterday afternoon my secretary left for Old Point Comfort. I don't eat here habitually so my coming to Hogan's wasn't predictable by anyone who knows me. That leaves it at you following me here. From my office. I suppose there's a reason, your own reason, but it interests me less than the secret of pistachio fudge. Three blocks from here I've got a boat that's begging to be put under sail. The week-end's one-fourth shot already, and what's left of it is going to be nice and peaceful and un-devious. So adios, as they say in your country. Some other time, perhaps."

I turned away, but her hand was on my wrist. "All right," she said, "I followed you here. Because first I wanted to see what you looked like."

"Over pie and coffee?" I suggested. "Like Dagwood?"

"Oh, please don't be sarcastic. I've had about all I can take. Jean told me about you, said you could help me. That's why I'm here. I need help, Mr. Bentley, I need it badly. My father—I—well, there's some trouble and we—"

I looked down at her. "You're just a trifle confused. You or Jean or both of you. I'm a tax consultant. I'm admitted to Tax Court practice but I'm not a lawyer. I'm not a cop or a private detective. The way it sounds that's what you want. Well, Artie Von Amond's reliable. He's got an office on New York Avenue, he's in the book. So—"

Her eyes stopped me. Cold. She lifted her purse, fumbled inside, and pulled out two crumpled bills. She pushed them toward me and I saw that each bill was worth five hundred dollars. She said, "Here's a thousand dollars, Mr. Bentley. There's more where it came from. Will you—?"

"Your husband's a lawyer," I interrupted. "Paul Sewall. Mouthpiece for Vance Bodine, the District's gambling king. Why shouldn't Sewall get someone for you?"

Her face had frozen. Her lips moved stiffly. "We've separated," she said. "Nearly a year ago. For reasons that don't concern you or anyone. Jean was at the affair last night. I'd had enough to drink that I had to talk to someone, so I told Jean in general terms what I wanted done. She suggested you. Said you were completely trustworthy, and told me something about you. Enough to convince me I should see you, talk to you."

"What did she tell you?"

"The Korea business, for one thing. The black market rings you broke up over there. Then a little about when you were with the Treasury, the way you got evidence for big tax cases. She described you to me: on the handsome side, highly intelligent, and with the social polish and discretion to handle an Embassy matter without attracting attention."

"Quite a build-up." I looked at the money lying on the table in front of me.

"Yes. I couldn't help wondering how she let you get away."

"It's a long story," I said. "And it happened quite a while ago. Ashes to ashes."

She glanced at the money, then at my face. "Don't feel offended because I'm offering you money, but I—"

"Money couldn't possibly offend me."

"Then help me," she said bluntly. "I know you've your own business to think about, but this shouldn't take you very long."

"For instance?"

"A week—perhaps less."

I took out my pipe, opened my tobacco pouch, and tamped mellow Latakia into the bowl. I lighted the pipe, blew a smoke ring toward the windows, and said, "Let's say I'm interested. Let's even assume I'll go all the way. But if you don't want publicity, I couldn't protect you if I slipped up or if something blew beyond my control because I'm not a private investigator and so there's no such thing as privileged communications between us. I can't offer you the same degree of security or privacy that a lawyer or a PI could. Do you understand that?"

She nodded. The waiter brought a frosted copper flagon to the table but I waved him away. I said, "You've sipped enough sauce for now and I want to be sure you've got a sober understanding of things. Just to remind you, the State Department runs a Special Detail to handle things quietly for foreign diplomats."

"I know. But that applies only to my father—he's the diplomat. I'm an American citizen. I was born in San Francisco when my father was a consul there, the—problem isn't anything he'd want the Department to handle or even know about. That's why I'm talking to you instead of my father. He was afraid to ask you to come to the Embassy, afraid to call you by telephone because of the talk it might cause among the staff. And if it should happen to become known that you're working for him, well, you aren't a private detective, and he can always say he was consulting you about investments or something like that."

My wristwatch showed three-fifteen. On my ketch the deck planking would be hot as a blowtorch but the beer cans in the galley icebox would have a delicate coat of frost. I studied the money, the two five-hundred-dollar bills a foot from my hand and thought of the new nylon sails and the new auxiliary engine those bills would buy. I blew a smoke ring upward, trying to circle the snout of a black marlin on the wall, still thinking about the money, balancing it against the lost week-end and the week ahead, and then I said, "I'll listen, Mrs. Sewall. But only if there's no obligation to buy."

She bit her lip and it seemed an oddly childish mannerism for the sophisticated daughter of a foreign ambassador.

"Very well," she said. "Now can we go somewhere and talk?"

I motioned over the waiter, paid for her drinks, and pulled back her chair. As she stood up, smoothing the iridescent silk across her thighs, she said, "Your boat's nearby?"

"You wouldn't like it. It smells of pitch and paint and there's oil and salt water in the bilges. Your dress looks like about two hundred dollars' worth of Garfinckel finery and it wouldn't ever be the same."

"Your office?"

"The air-conditioner's on the fritz."

"Well, the one in my apartment's working. I'll drive my car down and you follow."

I shook my head. "You might pass the balloon test, then again, you might flunk it. How far are we going?"

"Georgetown. Philips Place, west of Wisconsin."

"Where's your car?"

"On the pier. In the parking area." She took a small leather key-holder from her purse and handed it to me. "If you think I'm not sober enough to drive you're quite absurd."

"I'm just generally foolish. But thanks for giving in without a struggle."

Her hand picked up the two bank notes and tucked them into my pocket. They felt heavier than sheets of platinum. She slipped her arm through mine and we walked past the empty tables. As I opened the door the cashier turned up the volume of a hidden radio. The game at Griffith Stadium. The Senators versus the Visitors. With luck they might win a few this summer, I thought, meaning the Senators. With a lot of luck. The closing door cut off the cashier's chuckle. An out-of-towner, I thought. A Philadelphian. In Washington when the home team plays the natives seldom smile.

CHAPTER TWO

Her car was a red Lancia sportster. Right-hand drive with about six gear positions to occupy your left hand, and door armhole cut low enough to drag your elbow on the road. I had a hell of a time with the gearshift and finally she took over that part of it while I handled the brakes, the clutch, and the wheel. On the hard-top parkway heat waves rose like thin blue smoke. Ten degrees hotter and it would burst into flame.

People were sunbathing on the grass beside the parkway, flanked out limply on towels and blankets, or sitting with dark glasses drinking cokes and beer. It was a fine day for sunstroke, the best I could remember since last summer, and the season was barely under way.

I followed the parkway to P Street, turned west to Wisconsin, and stopped for a traffic light. It was time for her to shift, but nothing was happening. "Hey," I said, and turned to look at her, but her head lay back against the top of the seat and her eyes were closed. Her face was tranquil. I touched her hand. No response. She was breathing regularly, asleep in the sun. Asleep or passed out. The signal changed and I managed to mesh the gears. The Lancia purred up nance alley toward Philips Place.

Georgetown is new town, old town, poor town, rich town, dark town, light town. It lies west of Rock Creek Park and north of the old C & O barge canal. Its western limit is the wall of Georgetown University and on the north, Dumbarton Oaks. In early Colonial times it was a center of periwigged fashion and Federalist snobbery that lasted a hundred years. For another eighty the close-built dwellings settled and tottered apart until only Negroes would live there, eight to a room. Then for the last twenty-five the process reversed. The New Deal's flood of bureaucrats claimed Georgetown as its own. They tidied and rebuilt and improved and the politicians and financiers were attracted until with the exception of Foxhall Road it boasted the most expensive and exclusive real estate in the nation's Capital. On the fringes huddle morose colonies of dikes and nances, the shops and restaurants have names that are ever so quaint, and sometimes it seemed a shame that the slaves had ever left.

As for Washington, it has, per capita, more rape, more crimes of violence, more perversion, more politicians, more liquor, more good food, more bad food, more tax collections, more hotels and apartments, and more gold toothpicks than any city in the world. A fine place if you have enterprise, durability, money and powerful friends.

She hadn't given me the street number but it was listed on her car registration. The apartment was a one-story duplex. Not a reconditioned rat's nest like most Georgetown dwellings, or one of those precious little clapboard shacks, half-a-house wide and just big enough for a brace of mannish females who own a change of khaki pants apiece, a low-cost hi-fi and a record library heavy on the Delius and Stravinsky. Instead, the duplex had an honest brick face, Colonial brick and limed mortar, with horseshoe arches over the windows, and open wood shutters. The fence enclosing the lawn was wrought-iron painted black. Beneath the duplex was a sunken garage with room for two cars. I drove down the slanting cement apron into the garage and turned off the engine. Iris hadn't moved.

Getting out of the Lancia, I went around and opened her door. Draping her left arm around my neck I lifted her. She was not tall but she was solidly assembled. About one-twenty, probably less. Carrying her, I walked back up the apron, turned onto the sidewalk, and went up the brick steps. At the top of the steps a walk branched toward two doorways. Hers was solid wood, painted teal blue. In place of a bronze knocker there was an antique cast-iron medallion with a bas-relief fire cart and the date 1821 in flowing script. Typically Georgetown. The door key was in the leather holder with her ignition keys. I opened the door, closed it with my heel, and looked around for a place to put her.

Beyond the fireplace I saw a door. I walked over thick beige carpeting and through the doorway into a bedroom. It had turquoise walls, white woodwork, and lemon-colored curtains. The bed was Hollywood, double width, and the bedspread had foot-wide strips of turquoise and lemon. I lowered her onto it and pulled off her shoes. As I straightened, she stirred and murmured something but too faintly to hear. Her lips stayed parted and she looked as if she was good for at least eight hours. The room smelled faintly of expensive perfume.

I was hot and my back was weary from carrying her. For the last couple of years my exercise has consisted of carrying briefcases and tax books and running up sails. I left her on the bed and went back through the living room to the kitchen. All gleaming new, with copper pots and pans on pegs over the electric range. The refrigerator contained, among other things, six bottles of Danish beer. I opened one, tilted it, and walked back to the living room.

It was a big room, running the length of the house. Beyond the dinette picture window I could see a garden with lawn, flower borders, a couple of statues, and a miniature swimming pool. If it had been filled with beer I could have drained it in half an hour.

The furniture was Japanese style with foam-rubber cushions covered with shaggy beige cloth. The wood looked like black teak. On a chocolate leather hassock lay a Siamese cat. I looked at the cat and it yawned at me, stretched, and closed its turquoise eyes. Glancing around the apartment, I decided that the decor matched the cat.

Between the living-room and the dinette was a brick-and-wood half wall. The living-room side was a built-in bookcase. In one corner stood a hi-fi cabinet in dark teak. It looked like about fifteen-hundred dollars' worth of honeyed sound. At full volume it could tear the bricks out of the wall.

I sat on the beige sofa, sipped from the bottle, and put it down on the teakwood chow table. Against the far wall hung a row of Japanese prints. Ukiyoe. Beside the door there was a framed silk kakemono, a brush painting of a red-crested heron. Also Japanese. All very chichi. All very nice. You had an Oriental cat so you decorated your apartment in matching colors, and to avoid spoiling the effect you brought in custom-made Japanese-style furniture and silk paintings and wood prints. What else? If you had money, that is.

Picking up the bottle, I let the cold liquid trickle down my throat. It was excellent beer. I could almost taste ripe wheat.

No sounds from the bedroom.

I got up, turned down the air-conditioner, and sat in a different chair. From there I could see a silver-framed photograph on top of a tansu chest. The picture looked like Iris Calvo Sewall, taken a few years ago. For no particular reason I got up and walked over to it. The same nose, the same hair line, almost the same face. But written at an angle across the lower right-hand corner were the words: Always, Sara.

That made it her younger sister. I studied the face and saw that the lips were slightly broader than the lips of the woman who slept in the bedroom. And they had a childish, pouty look. The corners of the mouth seemed spoiled, even selfish. The little sister. She looked like a mantrap.

I turned and went back to the chow table, picked up my bottle and finished it. My wristwatch read three forty-two. Still time enough to grab a cab back to the waterfront, up sail, and drift down the Potomac the way I had planned before Iris Sewall braced me at Hogan's.

Reaching into my coat pocket, I pulled out her two five-hundred-dollar banknotes, smoothed out the wrinkles, and admired the engraving. I could drop them on the table, walk out of the door, and never come back. For a while I considered the idea and then discarded it. I had had a bottle of excellent beer at her expense and I had agreed to listen to what she had wanted so much to tell me. On top of that I told myself that I had been getting stale. Any action you can get out of a pile of tax returns and a shelf of tax books is strictly mental. And tedious.

I persuaded myself to linger over a second bottle of beer and if Iris still slept I would leave her thousand dollars on the table and walk out.

Just then the telephone rang.

I reached for it, then hesitated. If it was her husband he might not like hearing a man's voice in his wife's apartment, separated from her or not. And Paul Sewall knew some nasty people, hoods who would sap me for laughs, then break my arches for staggering. Then again it could be her sister, Sara. Or her father, the Ambassador.

Picking up the phone, I said, "Hello," but there was no answer, only an exclamation of surprise, abrupt and sexless, and the wire went dead. I lowered the receiver, shrugged, and decided I should have ignored it. As I walked away from the telephone I heard a key in the front door lock. The door opened inward and a bulky Negro woman stared at me. From one arm hung the strap of a shopping bag. A shock of celery leaves stuck out of one corner.

"Hello," I said.

She looked at me, then at the half-closed door, deciding whether to scream or come in the rest of the way. Finally she said, "Where's Mis' Iris?"

"In the bedroom," I said. "Sleeping."

"Huh!" she exploded. "You the genneman kep' her out all night?"

I shook my head.

"She drunk?"

"Ask her. And skip the Aunt Jemima dialect; it doesn't come natural."

Her eyes narrowed and she looked apprehensively at the bedroom. When she looked back at me she said, "Thank you. No one else ever noticed. How does it happen that you did?"

"I was brought up around here. It's been twenty years since the last minstrels."

"They die hard," she said. "Some employers wouldn't like knowing I graduated from Howard University with a degree in education, but teaching pay isn't enough to support my son and myself. Mrs. Sewall isn't the kind who would care, but all her friends aren't like her. You won't say anything, will you?"

"Why should I?"

She brushed past me and went into the bedroom. After a while she came out, carried the shopping bag into the kitchen and came back. "I hung up her clothing," she told me. "I'll give her a neck and shoulder massage to bring her around. It shouldn't take long, Mr.—"

"Bentley."

"Mr. Bentley. I've never seen you with her before."

"We just met."

The Siamese cat stood up and stretched.

"Ava!" the woman called.

The Siamese cat arched her back and sneered.

"Siamese cats," the maid said. "The smartest domesticated felines alive. And don't think they don't know it. I don't feed her now, she'll sink her teeth in my ankle and laugh like a fiend. Excuse me."

Ava followed her into the kitchen. I heard the refrigerator door swing open, the splash of milk in a saucer. When the maid came out she crossed into the bedroom.

I walked into the kitchen, opened another bottle, and watched the domesticated feline lapping milk noisily. From there

I turned on the hi-fi unit. Sound swelled through the room and I lowered the volume a little. The music was unfamiliar but I liked it. It soothed me and brought back a sense of reality that had started leaving me when I walked out of Hogan's with Iris Sewall.

At four-fifteen the Siamese cat drifted out of the kitchen, found a comfortable spot on the rug, and began cleaning her chops. The bedroom door opened and Iris appeared. There was color in her cheeks, her skin looked freshly showered, and she had on brocade lounging pajamas and velvet ballerina slippers.

"Sorry," she said. "Terribly sorry, and all that, but the drinks were obviously too many. That or the sun. Or possibly both. In any case, thanks for staying around." She lighted a cigarette and glanced at the hi-fi set. "Like my music?"

"Anyone would."

She came to the sofa and sat on the far end. Her hands moved nervously. She was drawing herself together, getting ready to say what she had to say.

"Someone called," I told her, "but when I answered the line went dead. Sorry if I've compromised you. Then again, it might have been only Sara."

"My sister? How did you—?" She turned toward the photograph and her face relaxed. "Of course. No, Sara will still be sleeping. She gave last night's brawl. Her husband is Wayne Cutler. Perhaps you know him?"

I shook my head. "I'm not part of the mallet-and-horse-show crowd."

"A worker who scorns the drones."

"If we have to put it that particular way, that would be a way to put it. Is your sister involved in this problem of yours?" I thought I'd help her get to the point.

"No—no, it isn't Sara. Not this time. And what made you ask? Do you know about those other times?"

"What kind of times?"

"Oh, when she was at Fentriss after me. Running away from school. The first time she made the papers she'd been gone a whole week. When the police found her she was in a Richmond hotel room with two sailors and a truck driver. Drunk. The next time it was a policeman in Alexandria, and so on." She blew a feather of smoke at the kakemono. "Sara's married now, so she's Wayne's problem, not mine or Father's."

The thread had given out. I gave it another tug. "An hour and a half ago you couldn't wait to tell me your troubles. You even gave me a bundle of earnest money. If you've changed your mind, I can still salvage something from the week-end. If not, why stall?"

She glanced at me, ground out her cigarette, and clasped her hands around her knees. Her ankles were slim and what I could see of her legs was tanned. In the room's semi-darkness her eyes seemed to glow.

Huskily she said, "It's a man. A man from Father's Embassy. One of the diplomatic couriers. His name is Silvio Contreras." She spelled it for me. "Tuesday night he brought a diplomatic pouch to the Embassy and the next morning he was supposed to leave with a pouch to Ottawa. But he never came back to the Embassy. Father is very upset. He wants Silvio found right away, and without any publicity. Silvio checked out of the Mayflower Wednesday morning and no one knows where he's gone to."

I took her money out of my pockets, laid it on the cushion beside her, and stood up. "It's a case for Missing Persons," I told her. "That, or the Department's Special Detail if your father feels it's something particularly delicate." I looked down at her. "Me—I think it's about as delicate as a blacksmith's appetite. He didn't run off with the Embassy pouch, did he?"

She shook her head. "Please—"

"—Or there's this one other thought: there's more than you've told me. A lot more. And I make it a point to pull out of anything that smells of flim-flam. Your story smells worse than a dead rat in a steamer trunk. I'd guess Silvio has something your father wants. Information, perhaps, or a letter or cash money. If you just wanted to find Silvio you wouldn't have taken the trouble of looking me up and handing me a thousand dollars; a PI could do it for fifty and show forty profit. Still with me?"

She nodded.

"Let's take it a step further. If Silvio's got something he should have given the Ambassador or taken something he shouldn't have, you'd want to get hold of it and you'd want it done quietly and discreetly—those are the words you used. Whatever it happens to be, you want it back. Before Silvio has time to pass it on or cash it in, or whatever else you're afraid he might do with whatever he has. Is imagination running away with me?" I asked.

Her tongue passed over her lips. Suddenly she stood up, went to the tansu, and opened the cabinet door. She took out a glass and a cognac bottle. She poured cognac into the glass, looked at it, and tossed it off. No cough, no choking spasm. Sauce was an old friend to this lady. As if I didn't know.

She refilled the glass, lifted it by the stem, and turned to me. "The effect was rather startling," she said in an off-key voice. "I don't believe in mind-reading, so you're as clever as Jean promised you were. And probably better." She lifted the glass to her lips, wet them delicately, and walked toward the sofa. Picking up the money, she brought it to me and put it in my hand. "I should have told you everything from the first. I shouldn't have tried to trick you."

"That sounds like a come on for more flim-flam."

"No." She shook her head and the hair brushed across her throat. "Honestly it isn't. Sit down and I'll start at the beginning."

Bending over, she took a cigarette and lighted it, all with one hand. Then she sat on the edge of the sofa and looked up at me. "Please sit down."

I sat down beside her.

She blew smoke across the chow table. The room was so quiet the air-conditioner sounded louder than Niagara Falls. Gazing at the end of her cigarette, she said, "You'd have no way of knowing it but my father's government has told him there's trouble down there. Agitation. Political trouble. You know how those things start."

"And how they end."

She nodded. "The Outs take over the government and then the Ins become the Outs. There's bloodshed and thievery and all the miserable rest. Well, it's been building up for a long time, and the government has been quietly sending a lot of money out of the country. Stripping the treasury, really, to transfer funds where they'll be safe even if there's a revolution, and where the funds can be used by the Ins if they become Outs. To help them become Ins again. The cash has been sent to places like Berne and Tangier and Hong Kong."

"The free-money markets."

"Yes. But none was deposited in the United States because of possible legal complications. I guess you'd know about that." She tapped ash from her cigarette. Her nails were almond-shaped, the polish blood red. Somehow I hadn't noticed before.

She said, "My father has been in the diplomatic service nearly thirty years. He's known and trusted. When his government started sending assets abroad they sent something here for his safe-keeping. Something rather special." Picking up the glass, she sipped cognac and set it back on the chow table.

"How special?" I asked.

She said, "If you know anything about my father's country, you know most of its wealth comes from mining. Copper, lead, silver, and gold. And gems. Some of the finest amethysts in the world are mined there." She looked at me sideways. "Do you know anything about emeralds?"

"I've never bought any, if that's what you mean."

"Well, they're the most expensive precious stone in the world."

"More so than diamonds?"

"Considerably more. Because they're awfully rare—the perfect ones. The best have a deep velvety green color. The Czar's Emerald is the largest perfect cut emerald in the world and weighs only about thirty carats."

"Worth how much?"

"It isn't for sale, but I've heard it's worth close to a million dollars. There's a much larger emerald crystal, though, still uncut, that weighs about fourteen hundred carats."

"Quite a chunk."

"If the wastage in cutting brought it down to a thousand carats, then at the same value as the Czar's Emerald it would be worth around thirty million dollars. But it is badly flawed."

The room was cold but my forehead was damp. I mopped away the perspiration. "Is this the emerald we're talking about?"

"No, unfortunately, because it wouldn't be marketable. It's known as the Devonshire Emerald because it was bought by the Duke of Devonshire. No, the emerald sent to my father is a National Treasure. It has an odd and ancient history. Some historians claim it came from Cleopatra's Mines on the Red Sea, others that it was found in Madagascar and brought to the New World by a Portuguese sea captain. In South America it is called "La Verde de Madagascar: The Madagascar Green.""

A burst of sound blasted through the duplex wall. Iris leaned back and pounded angrily on the wall. The volume lowered suddenly and she turned back to me. "Tracy Farnham," she said. "Another hi-fi addict. It's his quaint way of letting me know he's home."

"A friend of yours?"

She hesitated. "Well—a neighbor."

"Any other cute traits?"

"A few. He goes in for Yoga and health foods. And he collects old coins."

"I always inclined toward flint arrowheads," I told her. "Old coins usually went for pop and licorice candy. Well, back to the missing emerald."

"Yes. It weighs slightly under twenty-nine carats. It is flawless and its color is a deep velvety green. It is polished and step cut. It has been appraised at more than a million dollars. For a month it was in a small package in Father's safe at the Embassy. Wednesday, when Silvio didn't appear, Father opened his safe to make sure everything was still there. Everything was—except the emerald. Silvio must have taken it Tuesday night while he was at the Embassy. Father knows he's personally responsible for it and the fact that it's missing can't be made public because it would become a burning political issue back home. The Outs would scream that the National Treasury had been ravaged by the government, and they might even be able to use the issue to set off a revolution."

"If Silvio has the emerald, what could he do with it?"

"Have it cut into smaller stones here or in Europe, sell them, and live happily ever after. Or if his political sympathies happen to lie with the Outs he might even have stolen it to provide them with the issue they need. You guessed correctly that just finding Silvio wasn't a matter of life or death, but finding the emerald is."

"Other than the Ambassador, who could get into his safe?"

"Only the courier—Silvio. Father—everyone—trusted him completely. He's been a courier for years. Father shared the combination with him as a matter of convenience. Planes don't always arrive during office hours and it was much easier that Silvio could simply come to the Embassy at night, open the safe, leave the pouch, and come back in the morning."

"Sara?"

She shook her head. "Why do you ask?"

"Children have stolen from parents before. Do you know anyone not belonging to the Embassy who goes there a lot? To visit your father, for instance?"

She considered for a moment, and then she said, "There's my father's brother—Uncle Oscar. He's in business here in Washington, but he couldn't get into father's safe even if he wanted to." Her eyes seemed to cloud. "Am I under suspicion, too?"

I shrugged. "The story you've told me points to an obvious conclusion—Silvio was the thief. It's so obvious I thought I'd examine other possibilities—if you don't object."

"Sorry."

"What does Silvio look like?"

She looked up at the ceiling, then down again. "He's about two inches shorter than you, with cropped dark hair and a small mustache. How much do you weigh?"

"One eighty-four."

"Then he's twenty pounds lighter."

"Any moles or scars on his face? Got all his fingers?"

"Well, there's a small scar under his left eye, but it's a very old one and you'd have to be quite close to notice it." She lifted the cognac glass. "The suitcase he usually carried was tan leather, scuffed at the corners, with an accordion pocket on one side for shirts. Oh, and he had a blue canvas overnight bag. The kind the airlines insist on giving you. And he's twenty-six."

"You'll do," I said, admiringly. "I could have traveled a lot farther and learned less. Does Sara know about this?"

She shook her head, then her eyes lighted. "If you think it's a good idea, I'll ask her if she's seen Silvio."

"Would she be likely to?"

"No—but until she married Wayne she lived at the Embassy with Father, so she and Silvio knew each other and Silvio fell in love with her, even wanted her to marry him. It was all rather silly and impossible."

"Presumptuous," I said. "But even an alley cat can stare at a queen."

She resented it with her eyes. Finally she said, "Perhaps Sara has his picture somewhere. If that might help."

"It might—or your old locket photo of him would do just as well."

Her lips drew together tightly. "Meaning what?"

"Pull back the claws. The outrage act doesn't even rate a yawn these days. Meaning that if our Latin Lover was close enough to Sara to play house with her—or get large ideas about it—he was probably close enough to Big Sister to play for real. It could read like this," I went on. "You know as much about the Madagascar Green as the government caretaker, and enough details about Silvio to be his doctor. If Silvio happened to be nuts about you—which isn't unbelievable—he might have been amenable to slipping out the emerald at your suggestion. And it isn't just fiction that associates stolen gems with beautiful women."

"What a swine you can be."

I bowed a little stiffly. "So something goes wrong and Silvio doesn't get in touch with you. Because you're involved you don't want the cops digging deep—at least until you're satisfied you have no hope of recovering the emerald. So you circulate among your friends for a confidential investigator, pick up my name, and sic me after Silvio, not knowing what's happened to him, but suspecting he might have skipped with the swag." I paused. "It makes a nice little story, Iris. Like it?"

"I despise it."

"The cops might like it," I mused. "I've known some who would gobble it like pecan pralines. What would make them like it even more would be the knowledge of your estrangement from your husband."

Her lips formed an uncertain smile. "And how wrong they'd be."

"I wish I knew," I said. "So far I've only got my little toe wet but the water looks awfully deep—and dark. Maybe you knew Silvio no better than you said, then again maybe not. He's not around to say, and your testimony can't be accepted as entirely disinterested. See what I mean?"

"I see a rather vile estimate of my character."

"Who says you have any at all?"

I got up, walked over to the telephone stand and looked up a number, and began dialing. From the sofa, she said, "Are you going to take the case?"

"I've still got your money."

"Who are you going to call?"

"A friend," I said. "One who doesn't chase foxes or keep a pack of beagles or even hang out in Georgetown. So in your book he's probably small potatoes—a little man. But he's smart and reliable and resourceful and he earns his pay. Got many friends like that?"

She got up from the sofa and ground out her cigarette. "I have a splitting headache. So if you'll allow me, I'll retire. If you learn anything or if you require more money, I suppose you'll let me know."

"That's the usual arrangement."

Her velvet slippers moved soundlessly across the thick carpeting. The brocade slacks rustled expensively and the bedroom door closed.

At the other end of the wire the phone was ringing. After a while a voice answered. "Artie," I said, "are you sober enough to do an hour's work?"

"If money's involved."

I gave him Silvio's description, including everything Iris had told me. It seemed like a lot to go on. I said so and Artie agreed with me. He would check hotels, motels, and rooming houses. National Airport, Union Station, bus terminals, and U-Drive-Its. For twenty-five dollars it seemed like very little work. Artie disagreed with me. On principal. When he had anything to report he would call my apartment.

I replaced the phone, glanced at Ava drowsing on her matching hassock, and began walking toward the front door.

Just then the hi-fi next door began blasting like a calliope. Tracy Farnham up to his little pranks. Maybe he was signaling to his playmate, the lady Iris.

As I closed the door behind me I heard Iris hammering on the wall. Lovely. A lovely relationship indeed. Waiting on the curb for a taxi, I thought about Silvio Contreras and the missing emerald. A million dollars was a lot of coin to be kicking around town in such a small package, and a thousand dollars didn't seem like much to pay for getting it back where it belonged. Slave labor.

It looked like Silvio, all right. Open and shut. As definite as Magnetic North. But the very obviousness troubled me. I could imagine Silvio opening the safe, taking out the Madagascar Green. But for whom? Himself? Iris? Sister Sara?

A taxi stopped and took me back to Hogan's for my car.

At eight o'clock I was in my apartment reading a book on gems. The telephone rang and it was Artie. He had located the taxi driver who took a man generally answering Silvio's description from the Mayflower to a dump on the east side, Chinatown. The Hotel Flora. There the desk clerk said the man spoke English with an accent and had signed the register as Samuel Cooper. He had not left his room all day.

I dropped the book and ran for the elevator. My Olds was parked in the basement garage, and besides, a cabbie would know the shortcuts to Chinatown. I made it to the Hotel Flora in under ten minutes and Artie was outside, lounging under a street lamp trying to look casual. We walked up to the desk together. The Flora was a three-story fleabag with worn wooden stairs.

For one dollar the snaggle-toothed clerk lent us the master key so that we could surprise an old friend. Artie and I went up the steps to the second floor, turned down a corridor lighted by a single bulb and smelling of wood alcohol, sweat, and decay. I fitted the key quietly into the lock and turned it but the door was already unlocked. The door opened inward on darkness.

Artie's pencil light flashed around the room, found the switch, and I turned on the overhead light.

The room looked like a shipwreck. Bureau drawers were pulled out, one was overturned on the floor. Stuffing and feathers had been torn out of pillows and chair cushions. The tan leather bag was empty; clothes littered the room.

The bed was an old brass four-poster with a sagging mattress. What made the mattress sag was a man lying on it. His tie knot had been loosened and the shirt collar was open. He lay on his back staring up at the ceiling and his eyes were as cold as stones.

Above his forehead the short wiry hair curled like black caracul. The mustache was missing but the scar was there. It angled down under his left eye, nearly an inch long and almost the same color as the rest of his skin. And that was deathly white.

Behind me Artie said, "Is that the guy you wanted?"

I picked up the limp cold hand and said, "It was."

CHAPTER THREE

Artie said, "My God, a stiff! You didn't tell me I was heading for anything like this."

"Think I was keeping it a big quiet secret just for private shudders?"

"Well, no. So what happens now?"

"It was a fast trip around the track, Artie," I said, and fished my money clip from my pocket. I pulled out five tens and handed them to him. "The race is over. Go buy yourself some hay."

"Half of that's okay."

"Never argue with a man in a generous mood. Anyhow, the other twenty-five's for walking out of here and forgetting you ever came."

His eyes stared at the dead body of Silvio Contreras. Wetting his lips, he said, "If the cops found out it'd be my license. Not to mention the bond. That desk clerk could have made me on the way up."

"He stank like a wine cask, Artie. When we leave we'll go down together. If he says anything, the guest was asleep. Or passed out."

Artie's fingers scratched the side of his chin. "Okay, if you say so. What's here for you?"

"Nothing, probably." I looked around the littered room. Silvio hadn't torn it apart, someone else had. Bending over the body, I pulled it over on one side looking for a bullet hole or a knife gash, but there was nothing. I let the body roll back. It settled like a sack of wet sand.

Artie said, "Maybe he died in his sleep, a heart attack. It happens all the time."

"Not to guys his age." I moved away from the bed, stepped over the tan leather suitcase that Silvio Contreras had carried for the last time, and walked to the wash basin. It had a single water faucet and a small eroded bar of soap, now dry. On the shelf below the cracked mirror lay a safety razor and a blue leatherette box with rounded corners. Beside it stood a small bottle with an etched glass top. The colorless liquid smelled like grain alcohol. I replaced the stopper and opened the leatherette case. Inside, on the black velvet, lay a hypodermic syringe. The plunger was at the bottom of the barrel and the syringe was empty. I lowered the top, went back to the bed, and bent over the face of Silvio Contreras. The pupils of his eyes were needle holes. One of the alkaloid drugs: morphine, heroin, or cocaine. M and H were used in an alcohol solution. One of them had killed him.

His shirt cuffs were unbuttoned. Pulling up his left sleeve, I saw small scars dotting his arm from his wrist to his shoulder. I pulled down the sleeve and Artie said, "A hophead, huh? One of the bang boys."

"And a big bang kicked him off. All the way to the moon."

"He did it himself?"

"I couldn't even guess."

"Then let's get going."

"Two minutes."

Working fast, I gave the room another going-over: mattress, pillows, chair stuffing, drawers, even the shoulder padding in Silvio's coat. Mopping my face, I looked around the room for one last time. If the emerald had been there, it was gone by now. I wasn't even slightly curious over where it might be. The question was one for the police.

Switching off the light, I left the room behind Artie, closed the door, and polished the doorknob with my handkerchief. I also polished the desk clerk's master key and carried it down the steps between my knuckles. Artie went out of the front door and I flipped the key onto the clerk's ledger. Without looking up, he wheezed at me. The wine fumes were thicker than an Italian wedding.

Artie walked beside me to the end of the block and said, "You're walking out of it? Just like that?"

"Any better ideas?"

"From a pay phone I could tip the precinct."

"I'd rather you didn't. I was involved in finding him because finding him was supposed to be done quietly, without publicity. And there's also an angle you're better off not knowing about—connected with the client's reasons."

"If you say so."

A cab had spotted us. It veered toward the curb and slowed. I said, "If you're worried about his family, Artie, his prints are on file and by tomorrow afternoon he'll probably be identified. Then the story will be out. All I'm asking for is time enough to warn my client so that he can make other plans."

Artie said, "Don't worry about me."

The cab door opened and I got inside. "University Club," I said.

At the Club I got out, walked down to the Statler, and took a cruising cab in case I had been tailed by anyone, which seemed all too probable. I gave the driver the address of Iris Sewall on Philips Place.

As I climbed the brick steps my watch read a quarter to nine. It had been a long hard day and now it was quitting time. Tracy Farnham's apartment was dark but its mate was lighted and the curtains were open. Standing in front of the door I could see into the living room. Music drifted faintly through the glass panes. It was providing a sweet, romantic setting for the pair on the couch. Iris was stretched out on the sofa, a drink in her hand. Beside her, on the edge of the sofa, sprawled a man in a sport shirt. He was leaning over her, bracing himself with one hand. As

I watched, he leaned a little farther and kissed her. Her free hand reached up and rumpled his hair. The man smiled and kissed her again. I knew what Paul Sewall looked like, and this was not her husband.

I leaned on the buzzer and waited. No footsteps, no response. I pushed it again and this time I heard a man walking toward the door. He stopped just on the other side and called, "Who's there?"

"Delivery boy."

A pause. "We aren't expecting anything. Who the hell are you?"

"Not much of anybody, really, but you might open the door. Or failing that, tell Iris her hired hand's come back. With news."

The footsteps went away. I peeked through the window and saw him talking to Iris. Suddenly she sat up, brushed back her hair, and began arranging her skirt. He walked back to the door, the snub chain rattled, and the door swung inward.

"Come in," he said grudgingly. "I didn't know Iris was expecting anyone. She didn't tell me."

"Does she usually?"

As I walked past him his face was ugly. I heard the door close. Turning to the windows, I pulled the drape cord and the curtains glided across the front windows. To Iris I said, "That isn't really for me, honey, you understand."

"How careless of me," she said. "I won't make that mistake again, but ordinarily the neighborhood's free of Peeping Toms."

"Perfectly understandable. You and the night and the music, and what's a body to do?" I felt a little giddy. The wine fumes from the Hotel Flora, perhaps.

I turned and looked at her guest. He was stockily built, handsome in a weak sort of way, and his eyes were smoldering. Dark eyes and not quite enough chin. His ears stood out from the side of his head like the boy in the saloon picture captioned Me Worry? Not really as bad but I could see it was a standing problem.

I said, "Somehow, during the course of our afternoon chat, I got the impression that our business was on the confidential side. If my impression was wrong he's welcome to listen. Otherwise, shall we hold it to a two-some?"

She looked up languidly. "Tracy," she said, "would you mind leaving us for a little while?"

He grunted and began walking toward the front door.

"Have a jar of Yogurt and a few pushups," I called. "It'll take about that long."

"You go to hell," he snarled, then the door closed.

I turned back to Iris. She leaned forward, butted her cigarette, and lighted a fresh one. "Now would you mind terribly just saying what you have to say? Unless you just make a specialty of inconvenient entrances."

I went over to the wall and rapped on it. "Thick," I said. "Solid. But I'll speak softly in case Peter Rabbit's listening."

"Do that," she said, and began to laugh. It made her face even more fetching. When the laughter ended she said, "You might as well sit down. I have the feeling this may take a little time."

"Very little."

"You don't seem to get along with Tracy."

"I'm just not the neighborly sort. I wouldn't lend him a jigger of Cointreau if his prize soufflé depended on it."

"There's that side of him, yes," she said, "but any number of women know the other—to their cost."

I let that one drift while I took her money out of my pocket. "The ride's over," I said. "You'd better get yourself the law." I let the money fall on the chow table.

Her face went white. "What's happened?"

"He's dead. Deader than Jeff Davis. On his bed in a Chinatown flop. The Hotel Flora."

"How? When did it happen?"

"Last night. Today. Who the hell knows? Morph poisoning. Or heroin. An overdose, Iris. And it takes a big jolt of hop to kick a junkie all the way. You forgot to tell me Silvio used the needle."

Her voice was dull. "I didn't know." She stared down at the money. "So you're all through? You're walking out?"

I sat down on the sofa. Someone's highball was on the chow table. I picked it up and drained it. "Death changes everything, Iris. So far as the chase went I was with you all the way. If Silvio took the emerald, he's dead. He can't give it back and no one can make him talk. Not even the U. S. Marines."

She raised her face and stared at me. "You didn't find the emerald?"

Glancing down at the two five-hundred-dollar bills, I flicked one with my index finger. "The search had already been made. The room looked like a henhouse after a long night with the foxes. If the emerald was ever there, it's gone now."

"Someone took it from him."

"You're jumping at conclusions. Someone ripped the room apart looking for it. The emerald or something else. Maybe Silvio's private cache of happy dust. To a junkie a find like that would be a pearl beyond price."

Her left thumb was tapping against the edge of the cushion jerkily. She became aware of it and glanced down but the thumb kept on tapping. "The police—do they know?"

"Not through me," I told her. "We're holding out on them— me and the PI who found Silvio for me. Silvio's prints are on file—from visa applications at the Department. His body will be found, probably by tomorrow. By evening he'll be identified." I got up from the sofa, slowly and a little unsteadily. "That's how much time your father has to make other plans regarding the emerald. At that, it may be an overestimate."

"He'll be ruined," she said.

"He's a diplomat," I said. "Your father didn't get to be an ambassador without knowing how to handle himself. There may be some tense days ahead but I wouldn't get all distraught over what's likely to happen to him." I took a deep breath to steady myself. "That's my last piece of advice, Iris, and it costs nothing. Oh, yes, there were some minor expenses. Fifty dollars to the PI for finding Silvio and then keeping his mouth shut. Mail me a check sometime. The taxi fares and the buck to the desk clerk I'll charge off to business expenses next April."

She looked up at me, making an effort to gather herself together. After a while she said, "There's nothing that could persuade you to keep searching for the emerald?"

"Look," I said earnestly, "I'm not a detective, a strong-arm boy, or even a cop. I'm just a reasonably competent counselor on Federal tax problems. If you have any next spring I'll be glad to have your business. As for the emerald, I never heard of it. If a man's lying dead in a doghouse in Chinatown, nobody's told me and I don't want to be told. Monday morning when I read about it in the papers it'll come as a complete surprise. So in answer to your question, the reply is nothing. Nothing at all."

She uncoiled from the sofa and her arms reached across my shoulders. One hand bent my head forward to meet her lips and we kissed. Her lips were full and warm, tense and yet supple.

Finally she moved her head to one side and said quietly, "Nothing could persuade you? Not even this?"

I took her arms from my shoulders. "It seems a little too easy to come by. But perhaps I'm wrong."

"You son of a—"

I shrugged. "Even if I were interested I'd want something resembling an exclusive arrangement, only your promises wouldn't be binding. Not so long as Paul Sewall has any claim on you."

"He hasn't," she said. "He has no claim at all."

"You've been too long at the Fair, Iris. Get back to earth. If Rabbit Ears next door wants to play with fate, that's his problem. I'm not planning to make it mine. For all I know, the guy who killed Silvio knows my name, or saw me, or one of his buddies did. He might take it badly that I blundered into the thing at all."

Turning, I began to walk toward the door. The carpet nap seemed thicker than ever. I could hardly drag my shoes through it. It clung like quicksand.

Behind me she asked, "Where are you going?"

I turned, surprised, and looked back at her. "Home," I said. "With a pint of bonded and a Nembutal I ought to be able to forget all about Silvio by morning."

One finger touched the corner of her mouth. Slowly she said, "What about me?"

"That could be a little harder."

I turned the knob and walked down the path. At the bottom of the brick steps I turned and looked back. There was a light showing through Tracy Farnham's Venetian blinds. I thought about knocking on his door and telling him everything was all right now and he could get back to work on the beige sofa, but the steps looked too steep and I was awfully tired.

From there I wandered over to Wisconsin, feeling the moist warm air wrap itself around my face like a steam towel, hearing the monotonous throb of air-conditioners from the houses along the street. Against the lighter sky the maple trees looked like hangman's oaks, torpid with summer heat. Nothing was moving.

On Wisconsin I turned down toward the river past restaurants, silver shops, antique stores, and groceries that charge a fee just for looking around. As I walked I could smell money in the air and I was sorry that so little of it was mine.

At Martin's I stopped and got into a taxi. Then I went home and got into bed. Before I fell asleep the phone began to ring but I put a pillow over it and turned out the light. If Iris Sewall wanted Tracy Farnham removed from her premises she could call the Seventh Precinct. Rugged boys and only two blocks away.

At three-fifteen the door buzzer dragged me out of bed and I staggered through the living room to a table lamp and turned it on. Then I opened the door. A man rode me back into the room, a big man in an ice cream suit, a blue polka-dot tie, and a thirty-dollar Panama hat. Stepping back, he closed the door. He had thick black eyebrows and a sullen olive skin. He came toward me with rigid, strangled steps that suggested a vise around his hips. No vise, though, just the memory of a bullet-smashed hip socket. Tip Cadena, one of Vance Bodine's pressure boys.

In a mild voice Cadena said, "Try answering your phone, friend. It could pay off in friendship."

"Or a sore ear."

From his pocket he took a short nail file and began to push back the thumb cuticle. Without looking up, he said, "That was Paul Sewall calling a while back. Want to hear what he had to say?"

"Not particularly."

"He says to lay off, friend. Off the wife."

"He's way off the track, friend," I said.

"He don't think so."

"That worries me a lot. Any minute I'll start shaking all over."

"Easy, friend. I got no argument with you. Not yet. For now I'm just passing the word." He looked up and spread his hands.

"What's behind it?" I asked. "Or don't you know?"

He rolled back on his heels, balancing himself. His knees gave a little and his weight went onto the balls of his feet. Kidding around like a boxer in his corner, but poised and ready. He looked strong enough to break my back with his thumbs.

His head slanted to one side. "You want to know? Well, there's you driving her car home from the waterfront where you keep your boat, and leaving her place an hour later. Then you had to go back again tonight. So it ain't all just rumor, friend. It ain't no whispering campaign some old-maid neighbor dreamed up. It's all facts."

"The boy next door doesn't worry him?"

"Farnham? Not lately. It's guys like you that make him really grind his teeth: not too ugly, educated, and no question what side of the bed to sleep on."

"The lady plays too many games for me. Tell him that."

One arm stretched out and dropped the hand on my left shoulder. It was a big hand. The fingers began to play with the muscles of my shoulder. The pain was dull. Low pitch for now, but he could build it until I was screaming for mercy. When Cadena was a tank sergeant on Luzon he had pulled the head off a dead Jap to win a ten-cent bet.

I thought about driving my knee into his belly but he was fast and too hard. I would probably just break my kneecap.

The pain was crawling up the side of my neck, probing into my spine. I gritted my teeth and ducked out from under. He just stood there looking at me, a slow smile on his lips.

"Hurts, huh?" he said.

"It hurts and it makes me mad. Don't underrate me, Cadena. I'm not one of the hophead spooks you slap around for laughs."

His eyes studied me, deciding if I was bluffing. Finally he shrugged and said, "No, you ain't like one of them. The way it comes to me you're supposed to be smart. I told you to lay off the girl. So let's see how smart you are."

He dropped the nail file in his pocket, turned and walked toward the door, moving with those odd, ankylosed steps. Opening the door, he went into the hall. The door closed.

I went over to the liquor cabinet and put a fifth to my lips. Cold out of the bottle the liquor tasted like steel. I shivered. I wasn't planning a big drunk. Just enough alcohol to get the blood moving again, however slowly. Putting away the bottle, I thought about latching the snub chain in case Cadena had any afterthoughts. Only it seemed kind of useless. If he wanted in, he could poke his hand through the panel as if it were wet cardboard. Tough. But Vance Bodine's lieutenants had to be tough. If you gambled with Bodine and lost the bet, you paid and no argument. Nobody welshed and lived. And so Vance Bodine lived like a baron on a white-fenced estate in Fairfax County's lush bluegrass, gave bigger parties than a movie magnate, and collected tribute from his fiefs.

I thought of Tip Cadena and shivered again. He must have been tailing Iris today, watching the Georgetown duplex. Tip or one of his monkeys. Or maybe Iris was only part of the reason for this little call. Maybe Vance Bodine had assigned his boys to my tail at the Hotel Flora. After all, Bodine supplied people like Silvio with their kicks. Maybe Silvio was doing a job in repayment and here I was messing into a theft and a murder. Or I could be just dreaming up a lot of nightmares for myself. I sure as hell hoped that was all they were.

Turning off the light, I went back to the bedroom and sat down on the bed. Hogan's, I thought bitterly. Why the hell did I have to stop there for lunch when the icebox held plenty of cold cuts? Why, after all these years, did Jean Ross remember me as a fellow both reliable and discreet, and feel obliged to impart my name to Iris Calvo Sewall?

Keep out of the public places, I told myself. The office and the ketch, they're for you. Exclusively.

Lying back, I touched my numb shoulder. Gently. It would be a week before his prints wore off.

Finally the liquor began to work and I fell asleep.

Sometime during the night a big Siamese cat clawed its way onto the bed. Its eyes were milky sapphires and its fur was brushed silk. It curled up on my face. I tried to push it off but I was too weak, and so it lay there, smothering me until dawn.

CHAPTER FOUR

By eight the next morning, I was out of the apartment, the morning paper still unread. I could anticipate the headline: Asia going to hell on a sled. Or Europe. We were closer to war than ever before. Or we weren't. It was the second lead I was avoiding—the one probably featuring Silvio Contreras, late diplomatic courier found dead under what they call equivocal circumstances.

Driving to the waterfront, I got it out of my mind, rowed out to the ketch, climbed aboard, and secured the skiff to the buoy. Casting off, I ran up the jib and mizzen and swung into the channel. All the way to Hains Point I admired the cherry trees and the blue sky, and watched slate-blue jet fighters from Anacostia and the silver airplanes moving in and out of the National Airport on the Virginia side. The taffrail log showed eight knots and the light wind astern made tacking unnecessary.

I broke out a can of beer, sipped it, and let my fingers trail in the cool water. After a while I rigged a squidding line astern with the feather jig, not that I expected to haul in a white marlin, but it gave the effect of purposeful activity, in case anyone cared.

Off Alexandria I made some sandwiches, opened another can of beer, and took off my shirt. The finger marks were there all right, in Navy blue and gold. For that much school spirit I could have been an Annapolis man.

When I pulled in the line I found a five-pound catfish on the jig, half dead from neglect. I cut out the barbs and freed the fish, thereby losing fifty cents at the Wharf.

Around noon I anchored in two fathoms off Broad Creek and slept for an hour on the bunk. When I woke I felt better, my mind was clear and relaxed, and for two hours I tacked slowly down toward Piscataway Creek, smoking my pipe. Yesterday had happened too long ago to try to think about, or it had never happened at all. That way it was better. Tomorrow would see me active in the case of Collector of Internal Revenue vs McFadden Products, Inc. A four hundred dollar fee, win or lose.

As I thought it over it seemed inconceivable that I could have talked myself into all that had happened the day before. It must have been a summer madness of a special kind. Iris had been a beautiful woman with a husband and too many flaws, and there were easier ways of making a thousand dollars. If I had been aching for action, I had found it all too quickly. From now on I would satisfy that craving matching wits with government attorneys. Or maybe another war would come along.

The wind shifted, freshened, and I set the jib and reefed the mizzen. It was coming from the southeast now. Raveled clouds covered the sun and the water had lost its aqua sheen. To sail as far as Gunston Cove would be more labor than I wanted, so I came about, ran up the spanker sail, and started back up the Potomac.

It was nearly six when I reached the Yacht Club and needles of mist were in the wind. I loped into the bar room for a bracer. On my hands and face there was a light crust of salt, my cheeks burned from the wind, and I felt that I could face the week ahead. A William Holden picture was playing at the Strand; that and a New York sirloin at Cannon's would top off the day nicely. I changed in the locker room, went back to the bar for a refill, and heard the page boy calling my name. The bartender motioned him over to me.

"Suh, they's a lady up in the lounge askin' for you."

"Did she give her name?"

"No, suh."

"Is she a member?"

"Don' know, suh."

"Thanks, son."

I swore and finished my drink. For the love of Mike, Iris, I thought, hire another pony to pull your cart. Taking a deep breath, I went up the linoleum-covered steps and into the lounge. The channel side had a plate-glass window running the width of the room for spectators on race days and moonlight dancing.

Drops of rain were spattering the window and the steward had forgotten to turn on the wall lights, so the room was dim. I saw her in a corner with a cigarette and a magazine. She had on a candy-striped skirt, a matching blouse and rope-soled shoes. As I neared her chair she looked up and it was not Iris but the little sister. She put aside the magazine, and said, "Mr. Bentley? I'm Sara Cutler."

"I know."

"How—?"

"Your picture," I explained. "One you gave Iris."

She was at least four years younger than Iris and in the near darkness her skin had a tawny, feral quality that made you want to stroke it and listen to her purr.

Flicking ash from her cigarette, she inhaled and said, "I apologize for coming here, Mr. Bentley, but I had to see you."

"All this has a faintly familiar ring," I said.

"Yes, Iris told me about you. Only this morning, in fact."

"I'm sorry she did. Because she may have represented me as something I am not. I am a tax counselor; my practice is limited to tax courts and tax matters. I am not a detective or a marriage counselor or even a validator of questioned documents. My area of interest is extremely confined. I don't do Indian hand-wrestling, card tricks, knife-throwing, or many of the feats I seem to be popularly credited with. My office is on Sixteenth Street in the Washington Building, hours from nine until five excluding holidays, of which today is one." I took a breath and noticed an amused smile on her lips.

She put her hands together, poking the skirt between her knees, and said, "You're fascinating, Mr. Bentley. You are also funny."

"I'm not funny. I am, in fact, very angry with you. So please go away."

She laughed and rocked back in the chair. "Really very funny, Mr. Bentley. So formal and so put upon. But I came to you because you are said to be an expert in your field. You are a financial expert, aren't you?"

"That's probably an exaggeration. I repeat, for professional matters my time is yours beginning tomorrow morning at nine."

"Please sit down," she invited. "It's a very long way back to Warrenton. A few moments now would save coming back tomorrow."

The wall lights went on, giving an orange glow to the room. In the soft light her face was incredibly young. The self-indulgence I thought I had detected in her photograph was lacking—if it was ever there. Her eyes were as large as her sister's, and as I looked at her face the story about the Richmond hotel room, the sailors, and the policeman became the slander of a spiteful sister, envious of her youth and beauty.

I sat in the chair beside hers. "Go on," I said.

"Would you mind if I had a drink?"

"Not at all." I motioned to a waiter and we ordered Rhine wine and soda. A pleasant thought for a rainy afternoon. From the corner speaker music flowed: A Foggy Day in London. Also appropriate.

She shifted a gold charm bracelet, making it chime dully, and said, "My husband is Wayne Cutler. Wayne Chatham Cutler, to be exact. Perhaps you have heard of him?"

"Five goals," I said. "The Bermuda race. The Warrenton Gold Cup. A large estate in Fairfax County with a thoroughbred stable, gilt-edge real estate in the District, and a winter house in Nassau."

Her eyebrows arched. "My God, have you made a career of him?"

"No, but he runs to type. Out of Charlottesville, is he not?"

She nodded. "Married in his senior year."

"Ah, yes. A girl from the South Shore. Subsequently divorced."

"You're quite amazing. What do you know about me?"

"Only your name and finishing school."

Something passed across her face. Memory? Anxiety? Then it was gone. She said, "Wayne and I were married two years ago. At that time his financial inventory stood at nearly a million and a quarter dollars. About a hundred thousand of it in cash. Last week the bank notified me that my checking account was overdrawn. It was overdrawn because Wayne had failed to transfer money to it from his own account. When I asked him he simply refused to talk to me. Friday night we gave a party for our second anniversary, and this morning when the catering bills were presented he told me that he was unable to pay them and proceeded to get drunk. He is still drunk. Tell me, Mr. Bentley, in your opinion, what has happened?"

The waiter delivered the Rhine wine and sprayed seltzer into our glasses.

"Well," I said, "canceled checks would tell a story, and bond coupons can be traced. Real estate sales are recorded. An estate as large as yours would have a manager who keeps books. And tax statements always tell something. The laws being what they are, you can't dispose of much money without showing it somewhere. Is that what you want to find out?"

She nodded. "Would it be hard to do?"

"It would depend largely upon how co-operative your husband wanted to be. Or maybe he'll get up tomorrow morning, feel differently, and decide to tell you."

"He won't."

I leaned forward. "Are you in love with your husband?"

Her eyes moved away. "Well…"

"I wasn't asking just out of crass curiosity, Mrs. Cutler. Echoes of a financial search such as the one I've described could reach his ears quite easily, and in his position he might well resent it."

She looked back at me. "He would probably break my neck."

"That would be a shame," I said, and meant it. "Mrs. Cutler, I haven't yet taken the case. If I should, you would have to understand that I could offer you very little protection. If it came to Wayne's attention that I was looking into his financial situation and he charged me with it, the most I could deny would be the name of my client. And under the circumstances, don't you think he might have a pretty good idea you were involved?"

"He might, but you could also hint that Paul Sewall hired you."

"Sewall?"

"Yes—he's my brother-in-law, you know."

"I know." I ran my fingers through my hair. "Even if I were willing to go in for deliberate misdirection and such-like, would it sound logical to Wayne?"

She shrugged very slightly. "I believe it could. You see, Paul handles things for Vance Bodine and Bodine's had some business dealings with my husband."

"I see," I said, not really seeing, just getting the glimmerings of an idea. "Your husband gambles?"

Her face flushed and she said irritably, "Of course not. Vance is interested in Wayne's property—the estate and the stable. He's made him offers from time to time. Naturally, Wayne wouldn't consider it."

"Naturally," I said, "but that was before he ran short of funds. Suppose Bodine made him another offer—would he accept?"

"I can't believe he would," she answered, but there was worry in her voice. "The land has belonged to the Cutlers since before the Revolution. Why, some of the Aga Khan's horses have come from the Cutler stable."

I fished out my pipe and lighted it. "As a man who has seen other men go broke—completely broke—I find it quite possible to believe that the same thing has happened to your husband. Unpleasant, yes, but entirely possible." And also possible, it suddenly occurred to me, was Wayne maybe having something to do with the disappearance of the Madagascar Green, a rock that could bail him out of all his troubles. He had the connections and—

"I can't believe he's really broke," she said, interrupting my thought.

"You don't want to believe it. You want reassurance that you'll be able to keep on having juleps in bed, a high gloss on your Delahaye, and a servile darky to help you mount your chestnut jumper."

"Aren't you being a little insulting?"

"If I am it's because I have the feeling you haven't been completely frank with me, Mrs. Cutler—a fault shared with your sister. On further thought I think you know the money's gone, and I think you've a pretty fair idea where it went. Vaguely I glean an impression that you may want my services to substantiate your suspicions. Now men frequently spend more money than they should on two things—gambling and women. You say Wayne doesn't gamble, but most men of his background do. And as for the other possibility, I'm not going to inquire because I don't intend to take the case."

"Please ..." she said.

I stood up. "Sorry," I said, "but that's how it is. If Wayne's got a downtown wife, a PI can help you get the goods on him—if that's what you want."

"He has and I don't. Not quite yet. Her name, in case you're interested, is Janice Western. Not precisely from the Fairfax stud book but she seems to interest my husband. To the extent of having an apartment off DuPont circle at his expense. And a car. Plus charge accounts."

"Well," I said, "at least she's living in a comfortable part of town." I leaned forward and knocked pipe ash into a ceramic tray made to look like an abalone shell, thinking that her own casual conduct had probably provided her husband with all the reason he needed to play house with Janice Western.

I said, "Somehow the whole conversation seems to have deteriorated. To a point at which I'd better leave. I'm sorry you had the long drive in, but what you have in mind is a little too far off the beaten track for me. Yesterday I had one of your family excursions and it was a fair sample of what I could expect. If only people would stop recommending me I could get back to the kind of life I'm accustomed to. I don't want to be a supersonic test pilot, a member of an African safari, or the first man over Niagara Falls in water wings. So if my name ever comes to your mind again, please remember that. Better still, forget the whole thing."

Her hand revolved the glass slowly, and she said, "That is your final word?"

"Without any question."

The corners of her mouth toyed with a smile and she looked down at the amber-colored drink. "What would you say to ten thousand dollars?"

It stopped me. I stared at her and felt for the chair arm to lean on. My throat seemed suddenly dry. I waved my hand and said, "Please repeat that."

"Would you like ten thousand dollars?"

"Anyone would," I managed. "Only I don't believe there's that much money. Not lying around where I can get my hands on it. And certainly not to be made honestly. Not for doing what you've been describing."

"I am serious, Mr. Bentley. Completely serious." She glanced at her drink again. "And completely sober. I would pay you ten thousand dollars in return for a complete dossier of my husband's financial transactions for the last year. My reason for wanting the dossier would remain my own. Does the proposal interest you?"

"It's an interesting subject," I said, "but it's also a little unreal. Like table-lifting and spirit-writing. Somewhere there has to be a gaff. If I had the time it might be kind of diverting to find out. But I haven't the time."

"Why not? Are you afraid of Paul Sewall?"

"It's the people he knows who give me the shakes. People like Vance Bodine and his hired torpedoes. They don't just spatter gravel on your windows, they do heavy work, Mrs. Cutler—very heavy work indeed. And certain vibrations persuade me that Vance Bodine is somehow connected with your husband's plight. Last night I received a visitation from one of Bodine's heaviest workers just because I was seen driving your sister's car, or so he said. The marks are still on me. I'd rather not even think what might happen if Vance got the impression I was working at cross-purposes to him."

Her face hardened. "I wouldn't have guessed you were a coward."

"Let's just say I'm not anxious to walk under the feet of giants. So, thanks for the invitation, Mrs. Cutler, but no thanks." I slipped the pipe into my pocket and straightened my jacket lapels.

"I see," she said thoughtfully. "Since your mind is made up there is probably no purpose in discussing it further."

"None at all."

She stood up from the chair in a graceful silken motion, picked up her gloves, and did a mocking half-curtsy. "You won't—?" she said. "I mean, I'd rather you didn't—"

"—Spill the goods to Wayne?" I shook my head and looked around the room. "This place is touted as a gentlemen's club, Mrs. Cutler, Granting they may have stretched the standards in my case, I have no intention whatever of repeating our conversation or any part of it."

"Thank you," she said, and held out her hand. "I was unintentionally insulting. Please forgive me. And if you're ever around Warrenton, I'd be glad to buy you a drink."

"Thanks," I said, and watched her go.

Her walk was the same as her sister's. Co-ordinated, suave, and eye-catching. From a corner chair an older member cleared his throat appreciatively. I was with him all the way. In spades.

Out on Maine Avenue, as I ran toward the parking lot, I saw a beige-colored Nash-Healy pull into the traffic. It had no top and the occupants were wearing rain hats. Beneath the brim of one I saw the face of Sara Cutler. The man driving was Tracy Farnham.

Behind the wheel of my Olds I brushed rain from my jacket and started the engine. Guys like Tracy certainly got around. Georgetown one day, Warrenton the next. And somebody's wife each time. He was a real family friend. Or maybe I was exaggerating and there was a perfectly simple explanation for the whole thing. Maybe.

I didn't want steak any longer and the thought of Bill Holden's rippling muscles bored me. I drove out Massachusetts to my apartment, parked the Olds, and rode the elevator to the sixth floor. I broke out a tray of cubes, mixed myself a sturdy drink, and sat down in my favorite chair. The book on gems still lay on the floor where I had dropped it the night before. I picked it up, closed the covers, and laid it under the coffee table. A rush delivery from Brentano's for nothing. For nothing except a whirl around the carrousel and no brass ring.

For two days my blood pressure had gone up and down. I had found a corpse, concealed information from the police, and been kissed by the daughter of an Ambassador. I had even made myself a couple of enemies.

Tomorrow, Monday, I would return to my office and the niche I had carved for myself, and forget the whole thing—if Tip Cadena and his boss Bodine would let me. Silvio was dead, the emerald was missing, and an Ambassador was facing personal disgrace. His younger daughter's husband had stopped paying his bills and she was getting set to move in on him with writs and wherefores to cop whatever remained. After Vance Bodine had driven his claim stake, that was life in Ole Virginny and all terribly confusing. Unless there really was a connection somewhere between Silvio, the junkie, and Vance Bodine, lord of the manor house. Did Bodine have dope to sell—and did he pressure Silvio into heisting the emerald as a pay-off?

Outside the rain was spattering my windows and the dark evening sky looked bad for tomorrow. At that it might be a boon—if it kept the Calvo sisters home and out of my life.

I watched TV for a while, flicked it off and picked up the morning paper. The predictable headline was there but Silvio hadn't made the news. Tomorrow perhaps. Certainly by then the snaggle-toothed clerk would have found him and called the cops. And, of course, the search would be on for the two unidentified callers. Unless the clerk neglected to mention the loan of the key—and that was highly possible.

The wind and the sun had tired me. I turned out the reading lamp and leaned back in my chair. When I woke it was midnight and I had a stiff neck. I groaned and tottered off to bed.

CHAPTER FIVE

My secretary had sunburned arms and a blistered nose to show for her week-end at Old Point Comfort. At forty-seven, and a divorcee, she was still an optimist. The year before someone had told her that Marine officers from Quantico spent their week-ends at OPC, and during the season Mrs. Bross managed to go there at least once a month. So far as I knew she had yet to make a connection.

I had gone through the morning mail and got settled on some solid tax precedents when she knocked on my door and came in.

"There's a gentleman to see you, Mr. Bentley. Very distinguished-looking, if I may say so."

"You may. Name?"

"I—" She faltered. "Well, it never occurred to me to ask him—looking so distinguished."

"Successful con men looked distinguished," I told her. "Show him in, Mrs. Bross."

The man who came through the door had silver hair. It lay back from his high forehead as if it were engraved. He was a man in his early sixties and he wore a light gray worsted suit, a wide-spread collar, and a silver brocade tie, probably Italian. Holding his French cuffs were large silver links cut into a script letter. He was freshly shaved, massaged, and near one sideburn was a trace of face powder. There was something of the polished dandy about him. Maybe it was the pearl-gray gloves and cane that he carried.

But his voice was firm, even vibrant as he said, "Mr. Bentley? I am Juan Calvo."

"Ambassador Calvo?"

He nodded.

"Please sit down."

"Thank you." His pronunciation was perfect, but the Latin accent was there. Faintly. As he seated himself he half turned and looked questioningly at the open door. I got up and closed it. Then I went back behind my desk. He put his hands on his cane and leaned forward. "I appreciate your seeing me, Mr. Bentley—without an appointment."

"My work is largely seasonal," I said. "The slack period's just set in."

He cleared his throat. His eyes seemed to be interested in the metal airplane I used as a paperweight. He appeared to be having difficulty in getting around to the point. I let him work it out for himself.

Finally he said, "Mr. Bentley, I should like to express my appreciation for your assistance."

"You have," I told him.

"I have? How?"

"By coming here."

"Oh," he said, smiled, and reached inside his pocket. He took out a wallet and extracted a check. Leaning forward, he placed it on my desk. I looked at it and saw that the check was made out to Cash and signed by Iris Sewall. The sum was one hundred dollars.

He said, "It seems very little for your help."

"It isn't," I told him. "It's twice what I told Iris to send."

"Surely your time is worth something?"

"It was on a week-end," I said. "And then I had the pleasure of meeting your daughters."

"You met Sara as well?"

"By chance," I said. "At the Yacht Club. She came there yesterday to get out of the rain."

"She is my youngest—my baby. I love her very much. Not long after she was born her mother died. You will understand."

"Yes. Her mother must have been very beautiful."

He looked up at the ceiling. "I have never married since," he said. "No woman could ever replace her. With us it was that way—a perfect marriage—and I could never be satisfied with less."

"You were very lucky."

"Sometimes I feel that I was even blessed." He looked at me. "Mr. Bentley, the body of Silvio has been found. Late last night the police came to me. When the notice appears in the press it will be on one of the back pages, a paragraph or two, nothing more. The police have decided that he was killed by his addiction. And so there will be no scandal."

"That's good news," I said.

"The story satisfies you?"

I shrugged. "Apparently it satisfied the police."

"What disturbs you about it?"

I said, "They forgot to mention the room."

He nodded. "A shambles, I am told. Furniture overturned, pillows gutted. Everything to give the appearance of a search."

"It looked that way," I said, "because the room was searched."

"But not by Silvio?"

I shook my head. "By someone else. Someone in a hurry."

His fingers tapped the curve of his cane. "This someone—Mr. Bentley—could he have been responsible for Silvio's death?"

I took a pipe from the leather rack, opened a tobacco bowl and filled the pipe. I lighted it, blew smoke at the ceiling, and said, "Silvio killed himself with his syringe. He overestimated his tolerance and blew a hole in his heart. Isn't that what the police say?"

One hand made a gesture. "They were most helpful, the police. They had no wish to embarrass my embassy. If they thought otherwise they did not say so. What I should like to hear is your own opinion of the affair. Whether Silvio killed himself or was killed by another person."

I took the pipe from my teeth and leaned forward. "Mr. Ambassador," I said, "what little I know about drug addicts I learned as a Treasury employee. I am not a detective. I know very little about homicide or suicide. I tried to make that clear to your daughter. Any opinion I might have would be purely personal. A man is found dead from an overdose of a drug to which he has been addicted. The resources of the police are brought to bear and their verdict is death by misadventure. Even if their interest was lessened by the fact of the man's addiction, I am quite sure that the police would not conspire to conceal murder just to disembarrass a foreign embassy. You and I have reason to believe that the dead man stole something of great value from you. His room had been thoroughly searched and the object of the search is still missing. To me that would suggest that the injection was made forcibly, with intent to kill, and the room searched while Silvio was dying. Or, assuming part of the police theory, Silvio gave himself an extra big jolt because he was flushed with success and died as a result; the room was searched after his death by someone not responsible for his dying."

Calvo's lips had lost their color. He was no dandy now— he was an old man. His fingers trembled. "Who was that man, Mr. Bentley? I must know who he was. Whoever searched Silvio's room found the Madagascar Green, and I must have it back. My life—my career—depend upon it. Please—cannot you recall anything that would be of help? Surely you saw something that would suggest—"

"—who he was?" I shook my head. "Only this—drug addicts have to have a source of supply. The pusher could have gone to Silvio's room expecting to make a sale, found him unconscious or dead, and ransacked the place."

"A common thief would tear the room apart?"

"Well," I admitted, "it would have to be an uncommon thief. Abandoning that theory, let's return to the emerald—the thing you're mainly interested in. If Silvio stole it—and it's still only supposition that he did—he must have made advance arrangements to dispose of it. Worked out a deal to sell it to someone who could get it cut down and eventually sold, outside this country. Unless, as your daughter suggested, Silvio stole the emerald for the revolutionaries."

Calvo shook his head. "Unthinkable. I know the boy's family. Believe me—"

"All right, let's reconstruct: the man Silvio planned to sell the emerald to arrives at the Hotel Flora—the rendezvous previously agreed to—finds Silvio on the bed and searches the room for the emerald he had planned to buy. Or Silvio hasn't yet used the needle—he's saving that to celebrate the sale—but an argument develops and the purchaser jabs Silvio with the syringe, searches the room, and runs."

"With the emerald," he said faintly.

I held up my hand. "That's the big problem, Mr. Ambassador. The condition of the room is, only evidence of a search. It doesn't prove the emerald was found there or that it was ever there."

"But Silvio stole it," he said.

"Circumstances point to that, yes. Very strongly. Only the two of you knew the combination of the safe. But suppose the safe was opened by someone who did not know the safe combination?"

"Is—is such a thing possible?"

I relighted my pipe. "If your safe jammed or if you happened to forget the combination, you wouldn't call in a plumber with a blow torch. You'd get in touch with the manufacturer's local representatives. They'd send over a man who could open your safe in a couple of hours. Just by knowing how to go about it. I've seen it done."

He wiped his forehead with the back of his hand.

"While we're on it," I said, "let's examine one other possibility—that I took the emerald from Silvio's room."

"Mr. Bentley, I never—"

"If I did I would have been foolish to tell Iris when I located Silvio's body. Had I collected the emerald I would most certainly have walked out of the room and in a day or so told Iris I hadn't had any luck in finding Silvio. So, can we remove me from the list of possibles?"

"You were never at any time suspected by me or my daughter."

"I must have an honest face."

"You do. And your manner, it is also open and honest."

"A poor guidepost, Mr. Ambassador, but in my case, reasonably accurate. What we've done is exchange ideas, clear the air a little. What remains is finding the emerald. On Saturday your daughter gave me a generous fee to find the Madagascar Green. That night I returned her money and ended my connection with the case. I explained my reasons to Iris and she seemed to accept them. At least she understood them. I think I understand your position, Mr. Ambassador, and I sympathize with you. That's saying nothing, except that I mean it. Have you made plans to go on with the investigation?"

"No, Mr. Bentley, I had hoped that you—"

The shake of my head cut him off. "I take that as a vote of confidence from a man of discernment, but I couldn't handle things for you. In this country, and probably in yours, the information on which arrests are made comes largely from informers. I have none where the police have many, and every private investigator knows where to go for information of the kind you need. On Saturday when I gave Iris the name of a reliable investigator she shrugged off the idea, but that was Saturday." I wrote Artie's name and address on a note pad, tore off the sheet, and handed it to Calvo. "Mr. Von Amond is completely trustworthy, Mr. Ambassador. He doesn't go in for padded expense accounts or future blackmail. His services will cost you a hundred dollars a day, plus expenses—a nominal charge which buys you the time of a number of people. All professionals, and all experienced and equipped to help you as far as is humanly possible. Without being presumptuous I am recommending him to you. He doesn't need to appear at your embassy. He could meet you in a hotel room, a restaurant, or at your daughter's apartment. Privately. Let me suggest that you retain him in your behalf."

Calvo stood up slowly, a sick smile on his face. "I thought I might prevail with you where my daughter had failed. I see that I too, have failed."

"No," I said. "You've got what practical advice I can offer. I appreciate your reluctance to hire a private investigator—one thinks of them usually in connection with hotel-room blondes and errant husbands—but Artie's a good man. I suggest that you at least talk with him."

He shifted the cane and gloves to his left hand. "Perhaps I will, Mr. Bentley. And thank you."

We shook hands and I followed him to the office door. As I turned back my secretary said, "So distinguished-looking. Is he a client now?"

I shook my head. "Don't be impressed by outward appearances, Mrs. Bross. He was peddling party favors."

"A salesman," she sputtered. "Why, I never—"

"Neither did I. Next time better get the name."

"Why, I certainly shall, Mr. Bentley. Your time is much too valuable to be wasted on salesmen." She sniffed.

She was cosseting me a little, shielding me from the outside world and I liked it—in a pale sort of way. I went back to my desk, found my place on the page, and began reading again.

At twelve Mrs. Bross went out to take her place in line down at the cafeteria while I lingered over my work. I had filled my pipe and lighted it when a sound made me look up. A man was standing at the doorway, looking at me. About forty-five, medium height, a small mustache, balding hair, and skin the color of faded khaki. The collar of a figured sport shirt lay open around his thick neck. He said, "Mr. Bentley?"

"Yes?"

He walked toward me, fumbling in his pocket, and brought out a card. He held it out and I took it from him. On it was printed "The Fiesta Shop" in large letters. Below it, in smaller letters, the name "Oscar Calvo." Along the bottom was printed a Q Street address in Georgetown and a telephone number.

"Yes, Mr. Calvo?"

He cleared his throat and sat down in a chair. "You know my brother."

"Do I?"

He leaned forward. "The Ambassador. He was here a little while ago."

"He was?"

Calvo's face darkened, "Yes, he was here."

"Land sakes," I said. "All day long there's shabby gentility and dispossessed royalty and ambassadors and such-like trash milling around my office. Hell, I can hardly tell them apart. Your brother was among the throng? Well, if so, then what?"

Calvo's short fingers drummed the arm of the chair. "Mr. Bentley, I want to know what he came to see you about."

I leaned back in my chair and laughed at him. Unpleasantly. Calvo fidgeted.

Leaning forward, I said, "The day's filled with earnest seekers for truth. As for you, I don't particularly like your face, your manner, or even the way you dress. If the Ambassador came here just to pitch pennies I wouldn't give you even a mild hint."

"You would not?" he said in a dry voice.

"You've got it," I told him. "Just fine. So out of the chair and out of the office." I stood up.

He shifted in his chair and said, "Ours is an old family, a proud family, Mr. Bentley—"

"And you're the proudest one of all," I finished. "Oscar Calvo, a peddler of straw sombreros and armadillo baskets to dried-up spinsters. A proud and impressive representative of the Calvo family. What was it you were saying?"

In his face a nerve was working, under the skin and close to the jaw. It made his right cheek twitch a little. His face was getting red. He said, "There has been some small difficulty—my niece is involved. Iris." He took a deep breath, almost choked, and said, "Like most Latin women she becomes too easily excited. I am afraid that she has involved my brother in her worries. Juan—my brother—is a distinguished diplomat, Mr. Bentley. I am afraid that Iris's indiscretion—her excitability—might persuade him to do something unnecessarily rash. I would regret exceedingly if either of them had persuaded you to take up a trivial matter that could easily be blown up out of all reasonable proportion and became the source of unpleasant publicity."

"Go on with you," I said. "All that because your brother stopped by to check his investment portfolio with me?"

His face relaxed. Everything back to normal. "Then," he faltered, "then…there is no cause for alarm?"

"None at all."

He stood up quickly. "I apologize," he said in a strained voice. "Believe me, I am sorry to have troubled you. But my brother's career is important to me. A great man, Juan Calvo. Beside him, as you said, I am nothing at all. Do you understand?"

"Sure," I said. "No harm done—and excuse the acid tongue. Blame it on the heat."

Standing up, I shook hands with him and watched him leave. When the hall door clicked shut I sat back in my chair and relighted my pipe, but the smoke tasted like burning straw. A funny little guy. If failures are funny. I thought about phoning Ambassador Calvo to tell him that Oscar had tailed him to my office, but it seemed pointless. Oscar's motives could have been purer than diamonds, or there could have been a point I'd missed.

In any case the Calvos' problems were their own. If Oscar wanted to be the family watchdog he was welcome to the job. With my thanks.

Looking at my watch, I realized that on normal days it was time to put on my coat and walk over to the Occidental for a chop or a cold broiled lobster. Only today had not been a normal day. It had taken its tone from the week-end—from the Calvos. From morphine, emeralds, casual wives, and spendthrift husbands. Fascinating, if you had the time for it, but on an empty stomach just a trifle repelling. Like Tip Cadena and his pipe-wrench fingers. I shivered a little, and went down to the first saloon.

Over the jovial racket the bartender urged a vodka Martini, so I took one. Then another. Finally, my head swimming, I rode the elevator back to my office and got behind my desk.

Just then Mrs. Bross came back. She walked into the office and chirped, "I'm a little late, Mr. Bentley, but there was a handbag sale down the street and I simply had to get one. With the crowd and all I'm afraid it took longer than I planned."

"Think nothing of it," I said magnanimously and opened my eyes.

"Everything's been all right, Mr. Bentley? While I was gone I mean?"

"Hell," I said, "everything's been just fine."

CHAPTER SIX

About six, I got around to eating at a Mexican restaurant on upper Connecticut, but the arroz refrito had been fried several days before and the enchiladas had all the verve of wet blotter. The only thing palatable was the Cresta Blanca beer and of that I had several chilled gourds. Enough to temper my bad humor slightly.

From there I went to my apartment, just to check the place for termites, and ended by staring glassy-eyed at a TV puppet show. During a commercial break I realized how preposterous the whole thing was, switched off the tube, and decided to have my eyes checked for glasses before the week was out.

Picking up the book from Brentano's, I slouched into a chair and began to read. Emeralds, I learned, were comparatively soft, but highly brittle. They were one of the twelve gems worn in the breastplate of Hebrew priests, and were probably the equivalent of history's carbuncle. Acid and ordinary heat had no effect on emeralds, the book said, and in artificial light they retained their color. In their natural state they were found with quartz, dolomites, pyrites, and in mica and talc schist. The Greeks called emerald smaragdos, and the Arabs zumurrud. It was a fascinating collection of useless facts. Emeralds were an aid to midwifery, dysentery, and epilepsy. They preserved the chastity of young maidens—or rather, they were said to change color if the wearer was unchaste. And if that was not enough, emeralds were supposed to have the power of blinding serpents. Moore had popularized this superstition in a couplet that ran:

"Blinded like serpents when they gaze
Upon the emerald's virgin blaze."

A very high-flown sentiment, I thought, and turned the page.

The second paragraph was headed The Madagascar Green:

This ancient stone was brought to the New World by a Portuguese trader named Leão Bastos who used it to purchase Royal Patent to a part of the West Coast of South America in what is now Northern Chile. Here Leão Bastos lived in princely fashion until his death in 1572, at which time his land reverted to the Crown of Spain. For several years the emerald was worn in a gold necklace by the Infanta, but as Spain's fortunes declined the jewel was sold to finance further Spanish explorations in the New World. It is said to have been taken by Sir Henry Morgan at the sack of Panama and recaptured from his ship in an engagement with a Spanish vessel. However, nothing is recorded of its whereabouts until 1702 when it came into the possession of a Jesuit Mission located near Rio Sangre, as the gift of an Indian chieftain who had been converted to Christianity.

Since then the emerald has been part of the Tesoro Nacional where it may be seen by visitors.

Some doubt remains as to whether the gem was actually mined on the island of Madagascar. Although the volcanic Ankaratra range abounds in basalts and crystalline schists and many beryl quartzes allied to emerald have been taken from Madagascar, no emeralds are known to have been mined. For this reason, perhaps, the legend has sprung up that Leão Bastos obtained the emerald from Arab traders who frequented Madagascar and are responsible for the influence of Islam on that island. The Arabs, it is said, procured the stone by rifling the sepulcher of a Pharaoh—a regrettable practice and one still encountered in lower Egypt. Based on this slim supposition certain romanticists have referred to this emerald as Cleopatra's Emerald, citing Cleopatra's Mines, on the Red Sea Coast in Jebel Sikait and Jebel Zabara, as the source of many emerald scarabs.

It's weight is 28.84 carats. Its specific gravity 2.73....

I closed the book. Panama, Egypt, Madagascar—the Rio Sangre. The jewel had covered a lot of territory. It had even been sent to Washington, D.C., for safekeeping. Instead, it was in the possession of a thief—a thief who might have murdered for it. Another episode in its long legend of blood and theft. Wherever it went its value made it a catalyst of violence.

I pried myself out of the chair and carried the book over to the bookshelf to gather dust. The Madagascar Green. La Verde de Madagascar. Cleopatra's Emerald. It was too romantic for me, the terms were too large, the menace too heavy.

I yawned and decided to mix myself a nightcap. Just then the telephone rang. I walked toward it, hesitated, and remembered Cadena's advice. Picking it up, I heard the voice of Iris Sewall.

"Steve—Steve, thank God you're there. Please come over right away. Please hurry."

"Slow down," I said, "if there's a prowler rattling your window call the Seventh Precinct. They'll have a brace of burly Irishmen over there faster than I could reach the street."

"The police?" Her voice shuddered. "God, no. That's what I don't want. Please, please come!"

I glanced at my watch. "It's eight o'clock, honey. Much too early for nightmares. I'd guess you've just been tapping the jug too regularly, so have Jasmine there wrap you in some wet sheets and phone a doctor. After a shot of happy dust you'll feel a lot better."

"I am icy sober and deadly serious. What I need more than anything is a cold calculating brain and that's what you've got. If you don't come I'll have hysterics. Steve—I'm scared out of my wits."

"Mix yourself a drink," I told her, "and mix another for me. I'm on my way." I dropped the phone, went out of the door and down the elevator to the street. A taxi got me to Philips Place in six minutes flat. I took the brick steps two at a time and pounded on her door.

It opened and she stood aside to let me in. A tall highball was standing on the tansu. I picked it up, gulped Scotch, and turned to her.

Her eyes were a little wild. Her face had a deadly pallor and her hands moved distractedly. Whatever the reason, she was badly frightened. She walked to me, put her arms around my shoulders, and laid her cheek against my chest. I felt her begin to give way.

After a while I took down her arms and handed her a handkerchief. "What happened?" I asked. "Paul put the freeze on you because of Tracy?"

Light came into her dull eyes. "Tracy," she repeated. "Tracy?" and began to laugh. The sound was thin and brittle and gasping.

I stared at her. Then I slapped her cheek. Not hard, just hard enough to make her notice it, snap her out of the hysteria. Her head seemed to snap back into place. Her eyes came into sane focus, and she touched the spot of color on her cheek. "Sorry," she said absently. "Sorry, Steve. I'm a softie. Please help me—tell me what to do."

"About what?" I almost shouted.

"About that." Her hand gestured toward the duplex wall. "In there. In Tracy's apartment."

I put down the glass, went out of her apartment, and saw that Farnham's door was ajar. I pushed it open and went in. The apartment was dark and silent. I felt for a table lamp and turned it on.

In front of the slate-faced fireplace lay a man. He was wearing a blue mesh polo shirt, gray Bermuda shorts, high walking sox, and moccasin-welt shoes. He lay on his right arm, his left hand even with his bare left knee. On the slate fireplace apron a pool of blood had collected. In the dim light it looked like dark brown wax. Near it a fly buzzed.

Walking toward the body, I saw where the blood had come from. The throat had been cut. It gaped like a second grinning mouth with delicate red-crusted lips. Near the temple I could see a blue-brown bruise. The one eye I could see gazed sightlessly into the empty hearth.

The man was Tracy Farnham.

I turned and began looking for the knife. Against the white Ankara carpeting it would have stood out, but there was nothing there. No knife on the sofa or under the chairs or near the body. Clicking off the table lamp, I went back and found Iris sitting on her floor, staring at an unlighted cigarette between her fingers. Her hands looked like wax.

"When?" I asked.

She turned and gazed up at me. Disinterestedly. "When?" she echoed.

"When did it happen?"

Listlessly she said, "I found him that way. He's dead, isn't he?"

"He'll never nibble another soybean sandwich," I told her. "Let's get down to cases. You found him dead. All right. How long ago?"

"I called you," she said dully. "I called you right away."

"That was about eight o'clock. Where have you been all day?"

She inhaled smoke and let it trickle out of her nostrils. Against her tanned skin it looked like lamb's wool. "This morning I was in Chevy Chase. From there I went to a luncheon at the Kennedy. Afterward I watched a fashion show at Garfinckel's, met Paul for dinner, and came back here."

"What time?"

"A little before eight. I was feeling rotten, Steve. I wanted some amusing company and knocked on Tracy's door. It gave inward and I turned on the light and saw him. I remember screaming—ridiculous thing to do—and then I was dialing your number."

"Did calling the police occur to you?"

Her head nodded. She glanced at the Siamese cat and said, "I couldn't call them, Steve."

"Why not?" I asked harshly. "It's murder, isn't it? He didn't slit his throat, swallow the knife, and lie down to bleed where his rug wouldn't get stained. It's no ritual suicide, Iris, it's murder. Someone cut his throat. Why, I haven't the least idea. But even if you thought he killed himself—which you didn't—it was a police matter. It still is." I walked to the telephone.

Behind me her voice said, "Don't call them, please. Not yet. I have to ... think."

I picked up the receiver: "There's no thinking to be done," I told her. "This is automatic. When a man's murdered you call the police." I paused. "Or would you have a good reason why not?"

"Yes," she said in a raw voice. "There is a reason. The reason I didn't call them."

"Well?"

She took a deep breath. "Sara. Sara was with him this afternoon."

I put down the phone and walked back to her. "Think that changes anything?"

"I can't call the police, Steve. Not if Sara—" Her voice trailed off.

I said, "Look, lovely, a body is lying over there. Tracy Farnham's. Sara—I'm sorry she was with him but she should have had better sense. Her prints will be all over the place."

"I know."

"The trouble is," I said, "you have the idea Sara killed him. You may even know a reason she'd have for doing it. Rape is out, because I imagine she rapes pretty easily. Be that as it may, he was sapped before he was killed, then his throat was slit. The wound is deep and clean, no frayed edges. It takes strength to make that kind of cut. I don't believe you could do it—either you or Sara. Who killed him I couldn't begin to guess, and anyway that's what the police are for. Sara's prints will be there—well, so will yours. That proves nothing—only that he entertained ladies and those follies he's paid for. Put off calling the police a little longer and we'll have a harder time trying to explain. So get on the horn and call them. Now."

The front door swung open and a man came in. He looked at me, then at Iris.

"Get out," the man told me.

He was a powerfully built man, of medium height, with blond hair cropped short. He wore tortoise-shell glasses, a dark blue summer-weight suit, a basket-weave shirt and a solid-color blue tie with a pearl stickpin. Above his breast pocket the edge of a pearl-gray handkerchief showed. The bridge of his nose was wide and flattened, as if it had been broken too often and the bone removed. His short fingers were thicker than Corona Belvederes.

From newspaper photographs I knew who he was—Paul Sewall.

I said, "Simmer down. We were just calling the police."

He granted, his lips twisted, and his blond eyebrows furrowed. "You were what?"

"Calling some Law." I turned to Iris, "Now your attorney's here I wouldn't wait another minute."

Sewall turned slowly and stared at Iris. "You've got a tongue," he said, "and don't I know it. So you might just use it to tell me what's going on. What he's talking about?"

I said, "It's the neighbor," and gestured toward the wall.

"Farnham? What's he done?"

"He's gone and got himself killed, that's what. He's lying in there with his throat slashed. It happened some little time ago. Your wife seemed to think Sara was involved."

"Sara."

"She was with Tracy part of the afternoon. Listening to Casals, possibly. Possibly not. Your wife got home a little while ago and found Farnham dead. For no particular reason she called me. When you made your entrance I was suggesting that she call the Seventh Precinct."

His voice was heavy. "That would make you Steve Bentley?"

I nodded.

"Sara—she killed him?"

"Probably not," I said, "but Farnham's still there. Take a peek and decide for yourself. He won't mind."

He dried his lips on the back of his hand and glanced at his wife. "You couldn't have killed Farnham," he said thickly. "You haven't the integrity. I'm not hypocrite enough to pretend I'm sorry he's dead, but if Sara did it I'll see she gets the best defense counsel money can buy."

Iris stared at him, and said, "What about me?"

"You? If you did it, I'd throw the switch, darling. Remember that."

"I shall," she said in a thin, frayed voice. "I will bear it well in mind."

Sewall turned back to me. "I thought you got the message Saturday night."

"It was delivered."

"You weren't impressed?"

"Plenty. Cadena's an impressive boy."

"But you still had to come back, sniff around for more," he said.

I said, "I told you how it was, Sewall. If you want to argue about it..."

His curled hands relaxed. He plucked out the pearl-gray handkerchief and mopped his forehead. "Sorry," he muttered. "Shock, I guess."

From the sofa Iris drawled, "Go get him, Paul, he's your size—or does that make the difference?"

His face went white. His hands clenched but he did not look at her. Instead, he said to me, "You better move along, Bentley. I'll handle it from here."

I said, "The way you'll tell it was I here?"

"No," he said. "Iris and I came back here from dinner and found the body." He turned and gazed at her. "Together."

I walked to the door.

From the sofa Iris called, "Thanks, Steve."

I opened the door. "For what?"

Outside, the heat was heavier than wet cotton. I loosened my tie, tossed away the half-smoked cigarette, and began walking over to Wisconsin. Along the street the projecting air-conditioners looked like rumps perched on window ledges, their low vibration a threnody for the dead man. From one of the houses came the heavy beat of dance music—a dirge for drums. The maple leaves hung listlessly, an old stone horse trough by the curb was filled with last night's rain. I stopped, dipped my hands to cool them, and wiped them with a handkerchief.

The only car on the street was a dark green Lincoln convertible. The streetlight made the lacquer glisten like sea water. As I neared it I saw a woman's face inside, by the sidewalk door. When I was even with the car she peered out and spoke.

"Paul," she said. "Will he be coming out soon?"

I moved beside the car door and stopped. Taking out my lighter, I snapped it and looked at her face.

She was a blonde, under thirty, with hair drawn back tightly from her forehead like yellow taffy. Her penciled eyebrows arched high over her eyes. She had a small nose, even teeth, and lips drawn exaggeratedly large with dark red lipstick.

I cut off the flame and dropped the lighter back into my pocket. "Not for a while," I told her.

Her voice was cross. "He said he'd only stay a minute."

I shrugged. "You know how it is with a man," I said. "A few drinks and the minutes turn into hours."

"The louse," she said irritably, "We was going down to the play and already it's after eight-thirty."

I glanced at my watch. "So it is," I said. "Tell you what you do, honey, if you want to make points with Paul, get yourself a cab and see the show all by yourself. He'll get there as soon as he's free."

"But Paul has the tickets," she pouted.

"There'll be a scalper on the sidewalk," I said. "There always is."

She shrugged. "Maybe I'll just wait."

I shook my head. "Suit yourself, but it'll be quite some time. The cops are apt to drop around just any minute."

"The cops?"

I nodded paternally.

"For God's sake, why?"

"Someone got cut," I explained. "There was some blood. Enough to interest the police. So—"

She was getting out of the car. The door closed heavily.

"Well," she said, "thanks for saying it. Believe me, I don't want trouble with the cops."

"Nobody does," I said.

She stood up, tall and beautiful in a stagy sort of way, and said, "You work for Vance?"

"No."

Her eyebrows came nearly together. "Funny, I thought I knew you. Who are you, anyway?"

"A friend of the family," I told her. "His wife's family."

"Oh," she said, in a puzzled tone. "Then you wouldn't know me."

"I might," I said. "If your name was Janice Western."

Her lips pursed and one finger touched the side of her cheek. "How would you know that?"

"It's the kind of life I lead," I said. "Washington seems to be my beat. That and Warrenton. Surprised?"

"Yes," she said slowly. "Sort of."

"I'm kind of surprised myself," I told her, "because I thought you were supposed to be Wayne Cutler's woman."

The eyebrows arched sky high. "Brother," she drawled, "have you got it wrong." She turned, walked around the front of the car, and crossed the street. I could hear her heels clicking all the way to Wisconsin.

Crossing nance alley, I saw a squad car tear out of the Precinct House on Volta and head toward Philips Place. Paul Sewall had been as good as his word.

I strolled down to Q, crossed 32nd, and found myself staring at a dimly lighted shop window. Across the pane red letters spelled: The Fiesta Shop. The display was compounded of Indian serapis, rush baskets, fake Aztec figures, assorted tin ornaments, and leather belts set with silver and bad turquoise. Clay water jugs hung from the top of the window and from them depended strings of dried herbs and painted gourds. Oscar Calvo's little racket.

Peering beyond the display, I saw a small light in the rear of the shop but there was nobody inside.

I turned from the window, sorry I had chanced across it because it brought back the morning to me, the start of a very bad day. At 33rd Street a cruising cab stopped for me and I went on home.

Sometime after midnight my phone rang. It rang with forceful persistence until I got out of bed and answered it. The voice was Paul Sewall's.

"Bentley?" he said. "You use your head. I owe you something."

"For what?"

"For Janice—getting her off the scene. She was just telling me. You've got the right reflexes; you saved me some inconvenience."

I thought I could hear the clink of ice in glasses.

He said, "I guess I had you wrong. Sorry I sent Tip and all that."

"Sure."

"Well," he said, "I'd like to make it up to you. What's the figure?"

"No charge," I said. "Not everyone has to be bought."

"All right," he said quickly, "but if I can do you a favor let me know. Oh, as far as I'm concerned, from now on Iris is public property. We broke it off tonight. Clear field if you're interested."

"I'm not. How did you leave it with the police?"

"Smooth as glass. They'll kick it around—maybe someday turn up the guy who did it. But they didn't bother us."

"That's hardly a surprise," I said, "but I'm curious about one thing. Janice was with you tonight—I thought Cutler was paying her bills."

The voice laughed but there was an edge to it. "Maybe Wayne was, but that's all over. I hear he can't even buy chitlin's anymore."

"So I hear. And you've taken over?"

"Me? You're way off. Tonight I was doing Vance a favor. He was out of town so I was taking Janice to the theater for him. In loco parentis. Get the idea?"

"I'll struggle with it," I said.

There was a silence while he sipped his drink, and then he said, "Well, thanks again. See you around."

"Where?" I asked. "The morgue?" But the line had gone dead.

CHAPTER SEVEN

Tuesday and Wednesday were different. By that I mean I put in eight solid hours of work each day, laid off the light wines and beer and gathered in two new clients. They were not captains of industry, but where their next thousand or so came from was not a matter of crying concern. Altogether things were pretty satisfactory.

Tracy Farnham's murder had been a one-day splash. According to police statements the murder must have been committed by a prowler surprised by Tracy. Suspicious characters were being rounded up and questioned. A brief obituary noted that Tracy had been a 1944 graduate of the University of Virginia where he played varsity tennis and thrown the discus. He had been interested in real estate and was part owner of an interior decoration firm and a novelty shop that specialized in Latin American imports. That brought to mind Oscar Calvo's place, but the story didn't specify. He was survived by his father, who was a resident of White Sulphur Springs.

In three newspapers there was no mention of Paul and Iris Sewall having found his body; the discovery was attributed to a neighbor. Vengeance was in the hands of Homicide.

On Friday afternoon the telephone rang while Mrs. Bross was in the powder room. I answered it and a thin, refined voice said, "Mr. Bentley? This is Phil Devinney here. Secretary to Mr. Bodine."

"Mr. Vance Bodine?"

"That is correct."

"I see. What would Mr. Bodine want with the likes of me?"
The thin voice tittered. From the name I assumed it belonged to a male. I knew the type, though. It collected Spode china, doted on Koussevitsky, and restored period furniture with loving care. The voice recovered its composure and said, "I am calling, Mr. Bentley, on behalf of Mr. Bodine to extend an invitation to a small affair this evening. He asked me to apologize for such brief notice, but the affair was arranged rather suddenly."

"What is the nature of the affair?"

"A lawn party, Mr. Bentley. There will be a buffet supper and outdoor dancing. If the weather continues fair."

"It wouldn't dare not. Well, Phil, convey to Mr. Bodine, whom I have never met, my thanks for his thoughtfulness. However, it happens that this evening I am otherwise engaged."

Just then another voice broke in on an extension. It was a rough voice, hearty with good humor. A man's voice. The contrast was startling. It said, "Bentley? This is Vance Bodine. I happened to overhear the conversation, and when you refused I thought I might try the personal touch. Tell you what I've got in mind for tonight: I've been a little bored lately, and I thought I'd have a few friends over to cheer things up. I've been calling around on the spur of the moment and I've got a good crowd lined up. So I think I can promise you an interesting evening. Change your mind?"

"Well," I said, "maybe I could disappoint the other fellows after all."

"Thanks. From what I hear we should have met a long time ago. I'll look forward to seeing you. Any time after seven. Know the place?"

"I've driven by," I said. "It takes the better part of a day."

He chuckled, said, "See you," and hung up.

I wasn't quite sure why I had agreed to go. Except that an invitation from Vance Bodine resembled a command performance. His Fairfax estate was called Southwell and its broad acres disposed herds of Black Angus cattle, a dozen sulky horses, three or four trout streams, and more quail and wild turkey than a game refuge. This from occasional and conservative newspaper articles in which Bodine was usually referred to as a gentleman farmer. The few stories that mentioned his slight limp referred to it evasively, as though it had been acquired, perhaps, fighting Sandino in Nicaragua. The truth was that Bodine had caught a .45 Thompson slug just above the knee landing a load from Cuba on Chincoteague Beach. That had been twenty-odd years ago, but the limp was still there. This was from friends at Treasury.

After work I drove to my apartment, changed, and stood in front of the window looking down at the trees purpling in the setting sun, at the high white traceries of cirrus clouds, their lower edges coppered with dying rays, and wondered why I had been selected to appear at Southwell. It wasn't because of my youthful good looks, my line of brisk chatter, or any alleged intellectual gifts, and Vance Bodine could hire certified public accountants by the gross. Whatever it was it had to be related to Paul Sewall or his wife or Sara or Wayne Cutler, because they were the only people I knew who were connected with Bodine in any way. Except Janice Western, of course, and our three-minute dialogue in the dark was hardly the reason. Of course there was Silvio and the Big Green, but I had to hope Bodine wasn't a part of that. If he was…

For a big two days I had been allowed to pursue my lawful occasions, then Bodine had seen fit to put the clamp on me. Or maybe I was just exaggerating and he was about to offer me the chief bookkeeper job for Bodine enterprises. A wide-ranging job that included horse rooms, faro layouts, slots, punchboards, and numbers. The subornation of public officials and the evasion of Federal income taxes. The sort of thing every young accountant aspired toward.

I was lighting a cigarette when the door buzzer rang. Crossing the room, I opened the door and saw Iris Sewall. She made a half-curtsy and I said, "Well, well, it's big sister. Do come in."

Iris was wearing a flowing dress of sheer silk printed in muted water colors. The top of the dress was cut low and held by infinitesimal straps. She wore wrist-length gloves and carried an evening bag. At the lobes of her ears were small clusters of pearls. Her hair was parted on the right side and swept low over her forehead.

I said, "For a woman newly widowed, as it were, you look pretty sassy."

"Thank you," she said.

I mixed a Scotch highball and carried it over to her. She was lounging on the arm of a chair looking down at one white slipper, an insignificant affair, held on by a single strap.

I said, "I'm glad to see the Farnham affair caused you no lasting annoyance."

Glancing up, she said, "Should it have?"

I shrugged. "The other night you were taking it all rather heavily. But then, that was two nights ago."

She turned the glass and the ice tinkled lightly. She said, "I gather you don't exactly approve of me."

"Why gather anything at all? Leaving the missing emerald aside, I'd say you have no troubles worth mentioning. According to Paul you're calling it a day. Well, that should please you. Isn't it what you wanted?"

"I guess so," she said, in a distant voice.

"Well," I said, "that's just fine, Whither bound tonight? A rally at the Carlton, or would it be something more on the exclusive side?"

"I'm going where you're going," she told me. "To Vance Bodine's. I thought you might want to take me. Just for the sake of conversation."

"A pleasure. Then, too, you could show me the way. You thought of that, too."

She sipped her drink, rested it on the arm of the chair, turned one ankle appraisingly, and said, "there was one other thing, Steve. Father has the emerald back."

I stared at her, gulped a mouthful of Scotch, and wiped my lips.

"What?" she mocked. "No reaction? I thought that might provoke quite a flow of talented banter."

"Oh?" I said absently. "Sorry. A weevil was boring my tatey-poke but it seems to be quieting down. What was that you were saying?"

"The emerald," she said dryly. "It was returned."

"Well, now," I murmured, "think of that. And how did it all happen?"

"It arrived this afternoon in a registered package that was mailed from a post office in the North East part of town. So everything's all right. I thought you might want to know."

"Oh, sure," I said. "The tumult and the shouting die. Just like that. Putting us back where we started—or speaking precisely, a little before. Forgetting the brace of corpses, of course."

"Two? You mean Tracy was connected with the emerald?"

I spread my hands. "Tracy was connected with you, Iris. What I mean is that through knowing you I had the questionable pleasure of viewing two newly dead bodies. That's all. So far as I know, Tracy never knew the Madagascar Green existed, much less that it was missing."

She nodded.

I said, "I don't suppose you'd know how I happen to be included in tonight's guest list?"

"Through Paul, probably," she answered. "The other night you made quite an impression on him. Or so it seemed."

"Between recriminations," I remarked. "Well, all's well that ends well. I've wondered, though, why it was he stopped by just when he did. You had just dined with him. Was it some little thought he'd forgotten to put across?"

"In a way," she said listlessly. "At dinner we were discussing the divorce. I insisted that Paul pay all the legal costs but he held out. Later he changed his mind and stopped by to tell me. So I'll be leaving for Las Vegas in a week or so."

"Well, then," I said, "that seems to explain everything. And how typical of me to misinterpret a generous gesture." I finished my drink and put it down on an end table. "Well, we've got considerable prairie to cover before we reach the chow wagon."

Outside, the summer night had a fresh tang that you could almost taste. With Iris beside me in my Olds, I drove down Massachusetts, turned onto Wisconsin, and crossed the Potomac over the Key Bridge. The wind tossed her hair against her throat and she sat with parted lips gazing at the crimson sunset. I turned on the radio, found some dance music, and let my mind drift back to the Madagascar Green. How nice to have it back all safe and sound. What fun for the sender to go to the considerable trouble of taking it from Silvio just to wrap up and mail back to the Embassy. For what? I asked myself the question again. Why? Surely not because the thief developed a bad case of coffee nerves or because the law seemed to be closing in. Up until today it had been a clean breakaway with the goal line ahead and no tacklers. Why toss away a fortune like a burned match? I thought about it some more but the whole thing made even less sense. It looked phonier than a blind man counting greenbacks.

When I glanced at Iris her head lay back against the seat and her eyes were closed. She was as relaxed as a kitten in front of a warm fire.

That's a lot of woman, Bentley, I told myself. Have a care.

CHAPTER EIGHT

A quarter of a mile from Southwell, we had to slow to a near crawl because of the traffic ahead. Most of it was turning in between the high postern gates that marked the estate's entrance. The cars were big and expensive and new. A good many bore diplomatic plates.

Near one of the posterns stood a uniformed state policeman directing traffic. His partner was checking license numbers against a list on a clip board. He seemed to find my number without any difficulty, made a check mark on the list, and nodded in a bored way. I stepped on the accelerator and we passed through the gate into Southwell.

Ahead, a line of cars meandered over a white-lined macadam lane toward a knoll cluttered with boxwood. The knoll was surmounted by a large white manor house with a neo-Georgian portico and columns that rose even with the second floor. The house was a size between Mount Vernon and the White House. I could see people on the lawn, parasol tables, white-jacketed waiters, and at least two portable bars. A small, intimate affair, Bodine had said. Just a few friends coming over to relieve the monotony.

The parking area stretched away from the base of the knoll and in due course a man in a white cap relieved me of the wheel and gave me a car check. I said, "I came to the right place, didn't I?"

"How do you mean?"

"Well," I said, "I had the idea I was coming over to share a simple pot-au-feu with Mr. Bodine, but from here the crowd looks like Ringling's opening day."

"Yeah," he said. "That's what it sure looks like. And the drinks are free."

Iris put her hand on my arm and we began to walk the gentle grade that wound around past the swimming pool to the back of the house. Only it was really the front. From that side of the knoll you could see a lot of Virginia—hills, woods, grazing cattle, and even a river. A sparrow hawk hung listlessly in the darkening sky. A bat no bigger than a humming bird darted over one of the strings of lighted Chinese lanterns.

Near what I judged to be the service entrance stood a row of charcoal braziers. The cooks seemed to be broiling small steaks, ground sirloin, and milk-fed chickens. At another table a tall man in a chef's hat was tossing greens in a huge salad bowl, and the near-by bar was doing a rush business.

Most of the men wore white dinner jackets or ice-cream suits and there was a scattering of Sikh turbans, Egyptian fezzes, Van Dykes, and Svengali mustaches. A few dark-skinned ladies wore saris. A high percentage of the diplomatic corps was present. The citizens with paunchy bellies and nondescript faces I took to be Congressmen. Tall, well-gowned girls with cigarette trays were passing through the crowd offering cigarettes, cigars, and probably snuff if you had left yours at home.

A varnished dance floor had been laid down, an orchestra on either side spelling each other. The one playing was a Filipino mambo combination. Plenty of bongo drums, but muted, and a trumpet with a thin snarl that sounded like the young Harry James.

We snared drinks from a passing tray and continued our meandering. Men bowed to Iris, a few came over to kiss her hand briefly, Continental style.

She said, "Father should be here tonight. I expect he'll be feeling quite happy."

"With reason," I remarked.

"Oh," she said, "there's Sara."

Looking in the same direction, I saw Sara. She was in a strapless lavender sheath dress and she looked cool and collected. At her side was a man in a dinner jacket. The jacket was made out of what looked like raw silk in inch-wide contrasting stripes, something like a cricket blazer. His face and hands were heavily tanned and short black hair lay close to his forehead like a monk's bowl tonsure. His slow stride gave the impression of controlled strength. His dark eyes were set deeply above high cheekbones and his mouth seemed to have been set in a perpetual scowl.

"Wayne," Iris identified.

"He looks as if he could lick his weight in sharks."

"He keeps awfully fit. Riding, rowing, and a small gym in their garage. He's a pretty good boxer."

"He looks it."

"Yes. I hope Paul's not coming tonight."

"Why not?"

"Well, because Wayne's here. They aren't exactly friends, you know."

"Do I?"

"Oh," she said impatiently, "you drag everything out so. That's what's behind my divorce. Paul's crazy about Sara. Wants to marry her."

"How does she feel about it?"

She shrugged, "Well, she's married to Wayne."

"But that could change," I suggested.

"I suppose it could."

Beside us appeared a reedy figure in an egg-blue dinner jacket and a maroon string tie. He was as thin as a nylon halyard and I seemed to hear the flutter of tiny wings. He bobbed like a Japanese butler and cooed, " 'Evening, Mrs. Sewall. Frightfully glad you could come."

"Oh, hello, Phil. Do you know Mr. Bentley? Mr. Devinney."

He extended a limp hand. The bones were barely fleshed.

"I have," he said, "had the pleasure of a brief conversation with Mr. Bentley, but only by telephone. We're so glad you're here, Mr. Bentley."

"Yes. It looks like quite a scramble," I remarked. "But that's what an evening with a few friends so often turns into."

Iris was frowning at me. A thin-faced man with a dusky skin came over and said something to Phil Devinney in a language that made no sense at all, but Devinney answered effortlessly.

When the man passed on, I said, "What was that?"

"The man? Oh, he is the First Secretary of the—"

"—the language I mean."

"Hindi," he said. "Western Hindi," he added. "Urdu, actually."

"Yes," I said, "by all means be precise."

His fingers primped a lock of sandy hair. "In addition to other duties for Mr. Bodine, I also act as a translator and interpreter. I suppose I have a flair for languages. I speak the Romance tongues, German, Japanese, Mandarin, Thai, and Burmese. Also Baluchi, Bengali, and Swedish."

"It seems hardly enough. What about Gaelic and Cymric?"

"All in due course. Right now I'm absorbing Uighur."

"Hell," I said, "with your appetite you ought to be able to tuck that away by morning. Along with Bantu and the Hamitic dialects."

"You're a flatterer, I'm afraid," he said roguishly.

"So I am. Well, I can see how a fellow like you would have his uses around here."

"So Mr. Bodine seems to think." He glanced at his watch. "Mr. Bodine asked me to ascertain if you would be good enough to meet him in the gun room in half an hour."

"If you'll tell me where the gun room is."

He turned and pointed with an elastic arm. "Around the far side of the house. Its windows face the side lawn."

"I came unarmed," I said, "but I suppose I could send out for a Winchester—or perhaps that's not what he has in mind."

"Steve!" Iris warned.

Phil looked at me, bobbed again, and tripped away—a silly harmless nance, bubbling with social thrills and self-esteem.

Sara and Wayne were lost from sight. A boy in his twenties ran over to us, introduced himself to me, and took Iris off to the dance floor. I plucked another drink from a passing tray.

Beside me a voice said, "Good evening, Mr. Bentley."

Turning, I saw Ambassador Calvo. He was smoking a cigarette in a long, carved ivory holder that was slightly stained with nicotine. "Good evening, sir," I said, and we shook hands.

"Iris told you of the stone's return?"

I nodded.

He smiled expansively. "And so I can be myself once more. Dios, what a nightmare it all was!"

"I can imagine."

"I was nearly out of my mind with worry. Now it is only something to forget."

"Yes," I said, "Like Silvio's death. So I don't suppose it matters who took the trouble of mailing the emerald back to you. Or why?"

His lips made a slight frown. "Even if it did, what could be done to learn the details?"

"Very little," I said, "at this late date. But you must have wondered why the emerald, once stolen, was returned to you."

"I have indeed. I assume the thief was unable to dispose of the stone, unable to find someone to cut it into smaller stones that could be sold without arousing the interest that trying to sell "La Verde de Madagascar" would arouse."

"Not to mention the risk. I suppose you have the stone in your safe, Mr. Ambassador?"

He sighed. "Thank God, I have. And the combination is changed."

I said, "Would it be a great deal of trouble to let me see it sometime?"

His smile was indulgent. "Not at all. I should be very glad to show the stone to you. When would you like to come?"

"Tomorrow, if I may."

"About eleven or so?"

"Thank you," I said. "I've read enough of its history to want to see it and I'll probably never have another chance."

"It's the very least I can do."

A bulky lady in a dress drew him away and maneuvered him onto the dance floor.

Under the portico Vance Bodine was standing talking to half a dozen men. He was a head taller than any of them and he wore a rust-color evening jacket and a matching bow tie. His dark mane was silvered at the temples and the silver was probably the real color because he was over fifty. He stood erect among the sycophants like a lion tolerating lesser carnivores. One of them was Oscar Calvo. Free-loading and making classy contacts.

I walked over toward one of the bars and beyond it, fifty feet from the far edge of the crowd, I saw Tip Cadena. He was tossing something into the air with one hand, catching it with the other, and rocking on his heels and toes. He wore a double-breasted white dinner coat and a conservative black tie. He could have been a guest from the Italian Embassy or one of the South American consulates. Except for his eyes. There were streaks of light in them and he never took them off the crowd. I walked across the lawn to him and only when I was six feet away did he glance at me.

I said, "Watching the fun, friend?"

"Yeah. For unscrupulous persons who might try to snatch some of the jewels."

"With two cops on the gate," I asked, "And a list of license numbers? It seems like an unnecessary precaution."

"Vance don't leave nothing to chance, friend," he told me, pocketing whatever he had been juggling.

"Quite a crowd," I remarked. "Everyone fits but the working stiffs like you and me."

His cold eyes studied me. I got out a cigarette, lighted it, and moved in front of him. His mouth looked just a little worried. He said, "I been meaning to square it with you about the other night, friend. Turns out you were all right all along. According to Vance, that is."

My right hand lifted and touched my left shoulder. "I can still feel it," I said, "but hell, it ought to quiet down by fall. Oh, about squaring things with me—"

"Yeah?"

I slashed my arm outward from the other shoulder and I put plenty of strength into it. The half-open knuckles backhanded his right cheekbone and his head snapped to one side. He grunted in pain, dropped into a crouch, and I snarled, "That squares it, friend. Leave it at that or we'll clear the dancers away and have it out where everyone can watch. Including your boss." I rubbed my injured knuckles in the palm of my left hand.

The breath hissed between his teeth. Finally he straightened up, ran one hand through his hair, and fumbled with his tie. Across his cheekbone the marks of my knuckles stood out like white pearls. His mouth twisted and he said thickly, "Don't push your luck, Bentley. Not with me."

"You'd sap your grandmother for the price of a sundae," I said, and walked away from him. My stomach was cold and very hard. At the bar I bespoke a double Scotch and was halfway through it when a woman's voice cut through the music. "Bored, Mr. Bentley?"

I turned and saw Sara Cutler. Her lips held a trace of a smile and her eyes were smoky.

I said, "Bored isn't quite the word. And not calling me Steve just makes me conscious of my age."

She lifted a drink from the bar, touched it to my glass, and said, "Salud."

"Y pesetas."

"Many pesetas," she added, and sipped the drink. "You don't mind if I say I'm surprised to see you here?"

"I'm a little surprised myself. At first it seemed like a poor idea but Bodine was able to persuade me."

Her mouth was bitter. "He can be very persuasive. And very frightening. I guess he might be able to frighten even you."

"That's quite possible," I agreed. "How are things around the Cutler hearth these days?"

"By way of changing the subject?"

"Sure, just a device."

She looked down at her drink, tapped the ice with her index finger, and said, "If there's been a change I hadn't noticed it."

"Oh. That seems to exhaust the subject." I turned to survey the crowd. "Sort of an Arabian Nights setting, Sara. To you it's probably as real as tomorrow morning, but to me it has a sort of phony magic-lantern quality. I keep waiting for the Genie to escape from the bottle and start raising all kinds of hell."

"Then Genie's been out of the bottle a long time," she said heavily. "The problem seems to be how to get him back."

"You're speaking of the problem of Evil in general?"

"Weren't you?"

I took her arm and drew her away from the bar. We walked along a boxwood hedge and I said, "I haven't seen Paul tonight."

"Neither have I," she said tightly. "Am I supposed to want to see him?"

"According to Iris you're the real motive for the coming divorce."

"Iris," she said with bitterness. "Yes, she would say a thing like that. Without mentioning her particular contribution to it."

"That failed to come out."

"Steve," she said quietly, "I can't help it if men find me desirable, even fall in love with me. It's happened before, and I don't know what Iris told you, but I never led Paul on. I can barely stand to dance with him—he makes my flesh crawl. What she probably didn't tell you is the mistake she made marrying Paul when she was still in love with someone else. In time Paul realized it and resented it as any man would. That was the beginning. There have been other things—including the fact that Paul finds me attractive—but I wasn't the cause of their trouble, believe me. As a wife I've given Wayne everything he could reasonably expect, including loyalty. So long as I'm married to him it will stay that way. For years I was a child—a nasty, selfish child, Steve—but when I became a wife I found something called self-respect and I won't give it up easily."

"Then I may have a little good news for you—Janice Western seems not to be under Wayne's protection any longer."

Her eyes opened wide, and the effect was like exploding stars. "When…? she asked. "How…?"

"Bodine," I said. "The old lion's taken over. I thought you might like to know."

She took a deep breath and passed one hand over her forehead. "I see," she said huskily. "So it's not as though he gave her up of his own free will."

"I didn't get the details. Why not ask Wayne?"

She shook her head. "There's a little thing called pride."

"Love's gravedigger."

"Yes," she said quietly, "I suppose it is."

We walked on and there under a stand of oak trees was a white canvas tent. In front of it stood two painted banners. One, a human head in profile, sectioned and lettered with character traits according to phrenology; the other a hand, the lines of the palm accented and also lettered. A mitt camp, a carnival touch for Bodine's little soirée. The Romany trade.

Sara said to me, "The Swami hasn't shown up yet, but with your psychic powers you ought to be terrific."

"Pen dukkerin," I said. "Romany for fortunetelling. The second oldest profession. No, I've never practiced it. Besides, I left my turban at home."

She laughed gaily, a little artificially, I thought, and opened the tent flap. I followed her inside. Except for a wooden table and two camp chairs the tent was bare. Sara gathered her skirt, sat down, and placed her right hand on the table, palm up. I went around the table and drew up the other chair. I placed her hand on my left palm, passed my right hand over it, and bent forward to scrutinize the lines.

After a moment I began: "The hand, like the face, is an index of the soul, for is it not with our hands that we render good or commit evil? And who can say that therein the story of our lives is not closely revealed to those who have the power to see and read?"

The tent was hushed. From a hundred yards away the music drifted with muted ease. Sara's eyes were wide, her face intent. I went on gravely: "To the navigators of old the stars were the signposts that led to the seven seas. Unlearned as they were, these ancient men made use of the mysterious heavens to guide them on voyages that rolled back the veil of ignorance and superstition that shrouded the world from the beginning of time. Today it is given to a certain few to find in the faces and in the hands of men the hopes and fears that guide their lives.

"I see a girl—young, beautiful and motherless—rebelling against the bars of convention. I see her running away from school. There is a hotel room, liquor, the faces of strange men. Yes, one wears a uniform…"

Her hand clenched, her breath came quickly, then she relaxed and opened her palm again.

I said, "The picture changes. This girl lives now in a large, gloomy house. She feels lonely, frustrated, ignored by her father. Into her life comes a young man. He has dark hair, a thin mustache, and he falls in love with this girl." My fingers traced a line in her palm. "The name is coming…. I get the initial S. I see…" My eyebrows furrowed. "Ah…I see him alone now. He lies on a bed in a room far from the land where he was born. He is staring at the ceiling. His eyes are open, but his body is cold. He is…"

"...Dead," she gasped, wrenching away her hand. "Silvio. Yes, he is dead. Oh, God, how do you know these things?"

I intoned, "The hand, like a face is a ..."

"Iris told you. Admit it," she pleaded.

"My dear," I said, calmly, "you must have confidence. There is an inner eye that ..."

She rose slowly. "It's frightening," she said. "Please don't say anything more."

"Calm down," I said, pushing back the chair. "I was doing what every psychic faker does. A little air of mystery, some generalities, and finally the specifics he's collected if he's a smart faker. So don't let it bother you. If you go in for palmistry or phrenology I may have saved you some money."

She took a deep breath. "Yes. You were very convincing. But don't ever do it again, Steve."

I walked toward the tent flap to open it and her arm brushed my side. Stopping, I turned, and said, "So much for the Romany trade."

Then I put my arms around her shoulders and kissed her lips. She closed her eyes and clung unresistingly. Her breath was like warm perfume. I felt myself getting a little dizzy. Her arms circled me, drawing us even closer.

Opening her eyes, she said quietly, "Why did you do that?"

"For the usual reasons, I guess. Plus the fact that I'm a no-good scoundrel."

"No. I've known the breed and there's none of it in you. I should have known you before, Steve."

"I take that as a compliment."

"It was so intended." Her hand brushed hair from her forehead and then she opened the tent flap. "I'll have to find Wayne now," she said. "He's probably wondering where I've been."

"Let this be a lesson to you. Avoid swarthy Swamis in dark tents."

"I'll try to remember," she laughed. Then she was gone.

I took a deep breath, got out a cigarette, tapped the end against my thumbnail, and lighted it. When I was a little steadier I pushed the tent flap aside and drifted back to reality. My watch showed it was nearly time for my meeting with Vance Bodine. From the tent I could see the side of the manor that housed his gun room.

CHAPTER NINE

I began walking toward the side entrance, went up the steps, opened the door, and went into the gun room. I went over to the side of the room, sat in a leather chair, and crossed my legs. Stubbing out my cigarette, I lighted another and looked around the room.

It was paneled in knotty maple. On the walls were old hunting prints, dim in the bad light, and antique firearms were mounted against the panels. Matchlocks, arquebuses, flintlock pistols, and derringers. Colt single-actions, muzzle loading squirrel rifles, even an old saddle Krag.

Built into another part of the wall was a glass-enclosed gun stand. Its width suggested that it contained about twenty modern rifles and shotguns. I could see ivory lozenges set into hand-carved stocks, beavertailed forearms made of swirl-grained woods, and silver-chased engraving. Near the desk stood a hip-high globe of the world. A maple captain's chair had a red leather cushion, and beside it on a small table stood a crystal brandy decanter and four small glasses on an oval pewter tray. The setting looked like a color ad for a second-rate brand of blend whisky. All it lacked was the distinguished-looking financier with silvered hair explaining an antique French dueling pistol to one of his junior bond salesmen.

I heard footsteps outside the door and the financier with silvery hair entered. He stopped beside the doorway long enough to switch on a pair of wall Bullseyes, said, "Been waiting long?" and shook hands with me as I stood up.

"No," I said.

His smile was genial. "Like old guns?"

"Can't abide them. They've all killed someone, they have falsely romantic histories, and they're priced outside my range."

"Reasons enough," he chuckled. "Sit down, Steve. Care for a drink?"

I nodded and he poured brandy into two of the glasses. Handing me one, he said, "I appreciate you coming out here on such short notice. A mixed group tonight, as you may have gathered, but everyone seems to be having a good time."

"If this is a spur-of-the-moment affair, I'd hate to see something you really put your mind to."

"Well," he said expansively, "I have a lot of friends and enough money to do pretty much what I want. But you may know that."

"I had that general idea."

He opened his desk humidor, extracted a cigar, clipped off the end with something in gold, and lighted the cigar. His fingers rotated the cigar slowly and carefully until the end had an even red glow. The touch of the connoisseur. Blowing smoke toward the window, he glanced down at the cigar, and said, "I've heard a few things about you and what I've heard is all to the good. You're fast on your feet, competent at your profession, and you know the value of a closed mouth. Those qualities don't turn up all in the same package too often these days."

I said nothing; it was his show.

He sat against the edge of the desk and said, "It was helpful to have an extra man to escort Iris tonight, Bentley, but there was more than that behind my invitation. I'll assume you know something of my background so I won't labor the point except to say that I've gotten where I am by keeping my eyes and ears open and by being smart enough to hire the talents and loyalties of men who are alert and reliable. Men like that come high but they are essential in my business."

"That's a point we might spend a moment on, Mr. Bodine," I said. "Your business. Exactly what is your business?"

He frowned momentarily, then his mouth formed a sardonic smile. He said, "Making money. Let's say that's been my business, but it's not an end in itself. You're intelligent enough to know that, the world being what it is, money means influence, possessions, and power. Basically there are two kinds of human beings in the world—those who work and those who do not. Early in my life I chose the latter category for myself, and what with one thing and another I managed to become reasonably successful. Now, at my stage in life, money as such has ceased to hold further interest for me. What I am interested in, Bentley, is power. And that is how you come into the picture."

I wet my lips with cognac and listened.

Bodine went on: "This fall there will be a state election and one of the candidates will be Paul Sewall. There will be enough money behind him to assure his election. Most of the money will be mine. There is a law governing political contributions which is largely ignored, but which is still a law, nevertheless. Because of it airtight means have to be employed to conceal the exact sums involved, as well as the identities of persons who contribute more than the legal limit. In this case I am talking about myself. An accountant clever enough to perform that kind of bookkeeping is a man who would have the ability to become, say, budget director for the state, and all that it could lead to. You get what I'm driving at?"

"The picture's beginning to emerge," I said, "but it might be better to let it stay in the shadows. I'm impressed by the people you can summon here, by the manner in which you live, and by the plans you have for keeping up your interest in things, but I'm not your man. In a way I guess I'm flattered by your estimate of me because when it comes to hiring people you can choose pretty much what you want. You're smart and you're hard, both admirable traits at the right time and place, and you've come a long way from Chincoteague Beach. In your own fashion you're part of the American success story—rags to riches—and that's why so many people are willing to ignore your origins and come here to slop up your liquor and wolf your food. Hell, I'm here myself. The thing is, Mr. Bodine, I worked for other men long enough that I had to strike out on my own. I have my own business, I'm my own boss, and it's an honest, dependable business. When I want to take a week off I can do it. I don't have a fifty-foot yacht—I have just a small ketch lying off Maine Avenue—and in a couple of years maybe I'll have money enough to buy one a size larger. Life's full of compromises—you don't have to point that out—but any compromises I make won't include a big bundle of worry that each time the doorbell rings my caller's a law man with a warrant. Maybe a fellow could get hardened to it after a while, but in my case I doubt it. So that's the way I look at things, and after I've finished your excellent brandy the best thing I can do is thank you for the offer and drive back to Washington where I really belong."

He twirled his glass by the stem, lifted it to his lips, and drained the brandy. He put the glass down slowly, looked at me, and said, "I'm not used to being refused, Bentley, and at my age change comes hard. On the other hand I get a pretty clear idea what kind of a man you are and I don't think pushing you around would do me very much good in the long run. Let me say I'm sorry I won't be having you around this fall after the ballots are counted, but I'm enough of a gambler to know I can't win them all. So let's forget the conversation—as far as it went—and get back to enjoying the party. Mrs. Sewall is a lonely woman and she seems to enjoy your company."

He came toward me slowly, walking with his slight, distinguished limp, and said, "All the same, thanks for coming tonight. You're welcome here any time, Bentley, only I wouldn't try slapping Tip around anymore. He didn't mean any harm."

"Hell," I said, "I was only clowning myself."

He saw me to the portico door, we shook hands again, and I walked down the steps looking for Iris or Sara and wondering if Bodine hadn't been just a little too agreeable when I turned him down. I decided he had.

The dance floor had been cleared for a team of ballroom dancers. I found Iris at a table watching the floor show with a blond-haired youth in a plaid tie and plaid cummerbund. His mouth was slack from too many drinks and he stared at me irritably as Iris said, "Well, where have you been all this time? I've been looking for you."

"I'll bet. I had a chat with Vance, remember?"

The youth drawled, "Who's your friend, Iris?"

I looked down at him and said, "Whoever I am, sonny, I'm bigger and stronger than you. You may be the fencing master's delight but that doesn't impress me even a little, so watch your manners."

Iris's laugh tinkled delightedly. "Sic 'em, Steve."

The youth was making an effort to get out of his chair. I put one hand on his shoulder and pushed down. The chair went over backward, spilling him on the lawn. He picked himself up, his hands clenching and unclenching uncertainly, and I said, "Don't make a big coarse mistake, Rollo."

His eyes flickered at Iris, he wiped his mouth on the back of his hand, turned and stumbled off between the other tables. Iris stood up and put her arm through mine. "You're awfully unsociable," she told me. "but I don't mind."

"That's good of you," I said. "Putting up with my surly gaucheries and all like that. I can see how I'd be a burden to a sensitive woman."

"You're no burden to me."

"Who said you were sensitive?"

We were walking toward the end of the house away from the dance floor. The dancers had finished their act and the crowd was applauding. I said, "Tell me about Tracy Farnham. All I know is what the obit said. You seemed to like him. And Sara—well, the hell with Sara."

"He wasn't what he seemed," she said. "Not at all. He had no family, no money behind him. At Charlottesville he ran with a rich crowd that despised him. He wasn't even very bright, Steve. Oh, he could dress well, and he had a certain amount of taste— enough to go over in Georgetown, and he could talk amusingly, but he was really pathetic. More than anything I felt sorry for him. That's why I was nice to him. Really, that's all."

"You have a heart," I said. "I'd started wondering. What about Sara?"

Iris shrugged. "She liked him for an odd reason. Tracy admired her husband tremendously because Wayne was everything Tracy wanted to be and never could be. Sara's a little girl, Steve. Wayne's too much of a man for her. But Tracy was a pale image who would run and grovel at her beck and call. Do you understand?"

"I'm afraid so." I reached in my pocket, took out a handkerchief, and mopped my face. We had stopped in the shadows of some tall trees.

Iris said, "Where are we going?"

"I'm not sure," I said, "but I've had about enough. I don't really fit into the setting here. I'm not an ambassador or an heir to landed acres or even a tinhorn politician. You and your crowd are so impressed by Vance Bodine, wealthy gentleman farmer— well, I'll tell you what Bodine is. He's an ex rum-runner turned respectable with the help of money from gambling joints and political grafting and dope. And you know it as well as I do. His stated reason for bringing me here tonight was to suck me into crooked politics with your husband whom he intends to run in this fall's election. I turned him down."

She turned toward me and said lazily, "You're always angry and always talking. Why don't you just put your cotton-pickin' hands on me?"

Her lips tilted upward to be kissed.

I shook my head. "I'll tell you why. It's because too many cotton-pickers have been there before me. And because I can't see myself as part of the tack-room games program. The air's too thin out here, too rarefied for my plebeian blood. I might cut some fancy capers for a while but it wouldn't be long before I'd stumble and fall. At my age bones knit slowly, Iris, if they knit at all. Does that answer the question?"

For a moment I thought she might slap my face, but she just turned and began running back toward the Chinese lanterns. I shrugged and made my way down to the parking area. Phil Devinney could look after her; I felt she would be perfectly safe with him.

My car was blocked by about four others and when the attendant had sweated it out onto the drive I gave him a dollar bill and he touched his cap. "Leaving kind of early?"

"Hell," I said, "I got in by mistake."

"With cops on the gate checking license numbers?"

"It was a mistake," I said, "believe me. Even Vance Bodine can make a mistake."

I gunned the Olds and shot ahead, down Bodine's divided lane.

Out on the highway the air was cooler and a little fresher, it seemed.

I cut over Lee Boulevard, skirting Arlington Forest, and crossed the river on the 14th Street Bridge. For most cities it would be early but Washington had slowed to a quiet crawl. Only the guards outside the White House seemed wide awake. There were fewer cars than Scotch grouse on Massachusetts as I drove toward my apartment. I moored my Olds in the basement garage and took the elevator all the way.

Pulling off my dinner jacket, I undid my tie and pulled the gem book from the shelf where I had abandoned it earlier. There was a chapter I had ignored before, but now I turned on the chair light, pulled off my shoes, and began to read it.

When I had got what I wanted from the book I closed it, turned off the light, and let myself yawn. I considered a nightcap and a last cigarette but my mouth tasted like the bottom of Dismal Swamp and so I pulled off my clothes and went to bed.

CHAPTER TEN

It was Saturday and Mrs. Bross was off to Old Point Comfort again, her hopes bound up in a new summer hat and a bareback Orlon frock guaranteed not to wrinkle. The morning mail kept me busy until ten forty-five when I put on my coat, straightened my tie, and went out of the office.

From the Washington building I took a cab around DuPont Circle, veered up a side street, and got off in front of Juan Calvo's Embassy. It stood on a corner, detached from the other Georgian buildings around it, a wide, three-story brick house swelling with ivy. From a flagpole that slanted out above the portico hung a flag striped with the national colors and showing the coat of arms in an oval escutcheon. Around the circular driveway were parked cars with diplomatic plates. The shiny Rolls with the low license number was probably the Ambassador's. Just the thing for a ten-block safari to the State Department.

Walking up to the entrance I reminded myself that just a week ago, lacking a few hours, Iris had first braced me down at Hogan's. For only a week it seemed that a lot had happened. I went up the veined marble steps, pressed the door button, and thought about it. Iris, Silvio, Sara, Tracy. Vance Bodine…

A colored man in a white jacket opened the door. "Yes?" he said politely.

I gave him my name and suggested that the Ambassador was expecting me. He opened the door the rest of the way and I went into the carpeted hall. He showed me into a waiting room and went away.

The room was medium size and cheerful. On the walls hung several oil paintings done in bright colors. There were white slip covers on the furniture and a long mahogany table held an assortment of recent magazines. One contained color photographs, trade statistics, and tourist information about the Ambassador's country. The effect was a persuasive impression that it was an awfully nice place to spend green dollars. The only souvenir items you could not take back with you were human heads shrunk by up-country Indians. It seemed a grisly thought for such an otherwise pleasant place.

The colored man came back and said, "The Ambassador will see you, sir. This way, please."

I followed him down the corridor and at the end he opened a walnut-paneled door. Juan Calvo was seated behind a ten-foot desk, wearing the same carved cufflinks, and his aqua-colored poplin shirt had the sheen of fine silk. As I walked toward him he stood up and extended his hand.

"Good morning, Mr. Bentley," he said. "It occurred to me that you might have forgotten our engagement, but then you are an American. Prompt and efficient. Your country never ceases to amaze me. You know, I have lived in your principal cities almost as long as I lived in my native country, my daughters are both Americans, and I shall probably live here when I retire."

"Funny," I said, "I was thinking of retiring in your country. If you have the head hunters licked by then."

"I expect we shall," he said indulgently. "Well, you want to see the Madagascar Green."

I nodded and said, "I had one other question, Mr. Ambassador. It has to do with the young man murdered next door to Iris's apartment. Tracy Farnham."

His eyebrows lifted. "Farnham? I hardly knew him."

"I didn't think you were intimates, but a sentence in his obituary caught my eye. It said Tracy had some money invested in a novelty import shop. From the description it sounded like your brother's place on Q Street. Was the dead man associated with your brother?"

Calvo took up a gold-barreled pencil and began twirling it in his fingers. Carefully he said, "I believe he may have been—even though I do not know the details of my brother's business. Is it important?"

"It's probably just a coincidence."

Calvo's eyes regarded me curiously. He took a deep breath, shrugged, and said, "Well, I will show you the Madagascar Green, Mr. Bentley."

"Fine. Could I trouble you for a glass of water?"

Calvo pressed a button on his desk, got up, and went over to the wall. He opened a panel door I had not noticed before, and I saw the gray metal facing of a safe. It was an old-style safe, made in England or Germany. A heister with sharp ears and nimble fingers could twirl the dial open in the length of time it took to smoke a cigarette.

The butler opened the door, cleared his throat, and Calvo told him to bring two glasses of water. Then the Ambassador bent over and began turning the safe dial. He swung the heavy door open, took a key from his watch chain and opened a smaller inner door. Then he walked back to the desk carrying a small paper-wrapped package bound with green cord and blotched with red sealing wax. He cut the cord, peeled off the paper carefully, and laid back the inner wrapping of white cotton. From where I stood I could see a green stone half the size of a matchbox. Walking toward it, I saw the stone's deep velvety color, the step-cut ridges that reflected light from the window. Calvo's breath exhaled in satisfaction.

"Is it not beautiful?" he asked me.

Bending over the emerald, I said, "It's the first time I ever saw a million dollars outside the Mint."

He chuckled. "At least a million dollars. Such a magnificent luster! and without a flaw."

"Leão Bastos had discernment," I remarked.

"Then you know its history." He nodded reflectively. "Yes, there is almost something miraculous about the stone. Such a deep velvet color—it is beyond comparison."

The butler had entered silently. On the Ambassador's desk he placed an ebony tray with two crystal water glasses and went away. Calvo picked up a glass, sipped it, and set it down.

I took the other glass, drank part of it, and said, "When was the stone cut?"

"More than a hundred years ago. By a Belgian who lived in Amsterdam. A pity, in a way, because the methods of today could enhance its beauty even more. But only a brave artisan would dare to cut such a stone. Emeralds are only three-fourths as hard as diamonds and quite brittle. A false blow or clumsy handling and emerald shatters like ice."

"May I hold it?"

He nodded.

I put down my glass, picked up the emerald, and raised it to the light. In my hand it glowed like a green coal, without the hard brilliance of diamond. Plucking a wad of cotton from the wrapper, I dropped it into my glass and pushed it against the bottom. Then I lowered the emerald into the water until it was resting on the bed of wet cotton. I raised the glass toward the light and looked at the stone from an angle below the horizontal.

"What in heaven's name are you doing?" Calvo asked nervously.

I turned the glass slowly, watching the stone until I had examined all four sides. I felt my breath catch, and then I lowered the glass to the table. Lifting out the emerald, I blotted it dry on the rest of the cotton, stepped back from the desk, and said, "Looking at an emerald in water held against daylight is supposed to enhance its beauty. This was my one chance to admire the Madagascar Green, and I didn't want to miss anything."

"Oh," he said, relieved. "You must confess that what you were doing seemed rather mysterious."

I laughed apologetically. "I should have explained but I guess I got carried away."

"Quite all right," he said, "but in what way does water add to an emerald's beauty?"

"It collects the light and focuses it inside the emerald. In jewelers' display cabinets the lighting comes from several directions to give the same effect." I wiped my wet fingers on my handkerchief, took out my pipe, and began filling it with tobacco. When I had lighted it, I said, "I'm certainly grateful for the opportunity, Mr. Ambassador."

"It is I who am grateful to you," he said absently, as though murmuring pleasantries in a receiving line. "Did you enjoy yourself last night at Mr. Bodine's?"

"I had my moments," I said, "but I must have drunk a little too much. I found myself leaving before Iris was ready to go."

"She always enjoys herself at parties," he said vaguely. "Well, we will see each other again, Mr. Bentley."

We shook hands and I went out of his office. The butler was waiting in the corridor and showed me to the door. Oscar Calvo was just coming in. A clean sport shirt and starched whipcord trousers. When he saw me he smiled and said, "Mr. Bentley—you were at the Bodine party last night and I wanted a moment with you. But you left early. I was most disappointed."

"What was it?" I asked.

He glanced down, apologetically, and said, "I must have made a strange impression on you yesterday. You were quite right to protect my brother's confidences. Again, please accept my apology."

"Sure. Let's forget it."

His eyes raised, lifted to the oval escutcheon overhead. "A beautiful embassy," he remarked. "Worthy of my country. I am always proud that my brother lives here."

"You'll find him in a good mood," I said. "The market's still rising."

He bowed slightly and I went on down the steps. The air was a hot mask as I walked over to Connecticut and turned into a drugstore.

In a phone booth I fished a dime from my pocket and dialed Iris's number. Listening to the phone ring on the other side of town, I scrapped the plans I had half-made to board my ketch after leaving the Embassy and expose myself to the river's coolness until Monday morning. What I had just learned I had not wanted to find out, but the suspicion, once planted, had to be run out.

When Laura, the maid, answered I told her to alert Iris that I was on my way over with business that wouldn't keep.

At the counter I ordered a small coke and sat sipping it. Two heavy-chested girls in tight Levi's lounged by the magazine rack staring at horror books. Their jaws worked cuds of chewing gum and their eyes were glazed. As I paid my check I noticed one of the pages. An odd-looking visitor from another world with a globe-shaped head and electron-tube eyes was leering at a nearly naked girl strapped onto a table, with electrodes taped to her ankles and wrists. In one corner of the weird laboratory a caged ape was trying to pry the bars apart. Globe Head, it seemed, was seeking the Secret Life Principle, and would let nothing stand in his way, clothing least of all.

To the girl I said, "Back to your algebra. When you're a little older it'll be a big help to your husband in figuring a system to beat the ponies."

The girl's eyes popped open. "Huh?"

"Well," I said, "it was a thought for the day," pushed open the door, and flagged down a cab.

The cabbie took P Street all the way to Wisconsin, turned north through the holiday traffic, and dropped me at the corner of Philips Place.

Sunlight filtered down through the thick leaves and robins were busy filching worms from the fenced lawns. Figuring the cost of sod and gardeners in Georgetown, earthworms were worth easily a dollar apiece, but in Georgetown everyone ate well, even robins. It was the one place in the country where you paid a premium price for an old Negro hovel, only to tear it down and cover the lot with fifty or sixty thousand dollars' worth of Colonial masonry. You could call it the regeneration of the South or you could call it a screwball idea. Depending on your social consciousness.

Across the windows of the apartment that had belonged to Tracy Farnham the blinds were drawn. I knocked on Iris's door and in due course it opened and Laura said, "Please come in. She'll be out in a few minutes."

In the past week something had been added to the room, a Japanese dwarf tree in a jade-colored ceramic holder. Its gnarled branches made it look like a stunted ocean pine.

The Siamese cat crawled from under the sofa, crossed the room deliberately, and rubbed against my right leg. It meowed slightly, then left me and jumped onto its leather hassock. It blinked at me once and began washing its face. So far as the cat was concerned I was just another piece of furniture.

The bedroom door opened and Iris walked into the room. She had on dark blue pedal-pushers, a peppermint striped shirt, and cordovan loafers. Her hair was brushed sleekly and her makeup was fresh. In ten minutes she had done a lot with herself. But then, she had a lot to work with.

Glancing at me, she made for the cigarette box, extracted one and lighted it. Exhaling, she said, "I hardly thought I'd be seeing you again."

"Oh," I said meekly. "Me. Yes. I got a trifle impulsive last night, didn't I? Due to the unaccustomed surroundings, no doubt. Well, I'm my old self today."

"You got me up just to tell me that?" Her voice was coldly furious. "You came here for some reason or other and you might just as well tell me what it is. And, please, no stalling. I'm not in the mood."

I looked around the room. "It's the Japanese atmosphere," I said. "In this corner of old Nippon it's awfully hard to get to the point directly. Everything conspires against it. If we were in Kyoto we'd have the green-tea ceremony lasting about four hours and that would be the beginning. Next day we'd have a little sake and maybe a few geisha songs. On the third day, after sukiyaki or a tempura banquet, I'd start dropping delicate hints leading toward the business of the moment, and on the fourth day it would be your turn to inquire politely, if indirectly, what burdened my mind."

"Well," she said, "I have a miserable headache, as you can imagine, and I'd just as soon pretend this is the fourth day. So, what brought you here?"

"For one thing it's our anniversary. Hogan's, last week. Remember?"

"I remember," she said, and flushed. "Well, I'm not in the mood for sea food. Anything else?"

I gestured at the dwarf tree. "Very handsome bonsai," I said, "old, too."

"Oh?"

"Yes. It just happens to be illegal to import them, you know. Elm-tree blight or something like that."

"It was a gift," she said impatiently. "Steve!" she almost shouted at me, "Get to the point."

I shrugged and sat down. "Well," I said, "I was reasonably sure I wouldn't be particularly welcome here today, but I didn't let that keep me away. Who brought you back from Bodine's, by the way?"

"Sara," she said. "She stayed here last night; she just left a little while ago. And that fortune-telling stunt you pulled on her was an awfully dirty trick. How low can you get?"

"Pretty low, I guess, but at the time it seemed the thing to do."

Gesturing toward the duplex wall, I said, "Tracy's place looks like a padlocked massage parlor. Who's the next tenant?"

"God knows. Tracy owned his half so it probably won't be disposed of until his estate's settled. Are you interested in it?"

"I could probably handle the initial cost, but the upkeep on a snake ranch like that comes high. By the way, you didn't ever tell me Tracy had a share in Uncle Oscar's business."

"It didn't seem important." Her eyes looked dangerous. "Now for God's sake, will you—"

"Yes. Iris, I have just come from your father's office where he was good enough to open his safe and show me the stone that was returned yesterday afternoon. An admirable gem."

"I haven't seen it for years but I could never forget it."

"The Madagascar Green?" I said.

"Yes." Her eyebrows drew close together in puzzlement. "Isn't that what we're talking about?"

"That's what you're talking about," I said. "So far, I've only been discussing the stone your father showed me."

"The Madagascar Green," she repeated impatiently. "Steve, whatever's wrong with you today?"

"Shock, maybe. From what you told me and from reading I've done the Madagascar Green is supposed to be a single flawless stone."

"Of course it is," she said, but her eyes were worried. "You've seen it. So what?"

I gazed down at my drink. "Only this, Iris. The gem your father showed me is valuable, all right, but it isn't worth any million dollars. It's made of two stones cemented together. The top one is probably genuine enough, maybe even the bottom one, but the whole is made up of two stones. If that's the Madagascar Green, someone's been having a long laugh at your country's expense."

Her face had whitened. "You...aren't...joking?"

"It would be terribly bad taste. No, I'm quite serious. The stone your father showed me is what's called a doublet—two stones cemented together. Usually a doublet has one valuable and genuine stone—the crown—while the other, the base, is an imitation or synthetic or flawed stone of greatly inferior value. In the jewelry trade it's quite common, so long as the buyer is informed. After all, whoever looks at the base of a precious stone? It's done to make a small gem bigger or to enhance the color of an imperfectly colored stone."

"You know what you're saying?"

I nodded. "If the real Madagascar Green was sent your father for safekeeping it has since been replaced. It was a good gamble because the thief knew your father wasn't going to put it on sale and have it examined by experts. Once the stone was supposedly returned, he did what the thief anticipated—put it in his safe with a thankful heart. He never thought a substitution might have been made because he'd had nightmares enough while it was missing."

"You told him?"

"No," I said. "You handled things before so I thought you might want to handle it again and spare him the worry."

Her eyes narrowed. "You're not a jeweler. How do you know the stone's a—a doublet?"

"It wasn't hard," I told her. "The test's so simple that passing off a doublet as a genuine stone has probably never happened. If you think back to freshman physics you'll remember that when a ray of light strikes water it's bent in a different direction. The bending is called refraction."

She nodded.

"All right. It's refracted because light travels slower in water than in air. They have different indexes of refraction. Likewise, hardly any two translucent objects have the same refractive index. Precious stones each have their own index of refraction and it's just as personal a means of identification as a fingerprint. The Madagascar Green, for example, has a particular refractive index that probably no other emerald in the world can match. Unique. By the same token, two emerald slices put together and viewed from the side in water would show up clearly as separate parts—due to their separate refractive indexes. I put your father's stone in a glass of water and held it up to strong daylight. The oblique angle showed a flat inner plane, Iris. It was unmistakable.

If you don't believe me, ask any jeweler about doublets, then do what I did with your father's stone."

I took a deep breath. Her eyes seemed sunken, her tongue flicked across dry lips. I said, "Well, that's today's bulletin, so far as it goes. Either the Madagascar Green has always been fraudulent or it was stolen from your father's safe and the doublet sent back in its place on the assumption that your father would never detect the substitution."

"Who could have done it?" she whispered. "Who?"

"A jeweler," I told her. "Because making a doublet to resemble a stone as large and well known as the Madagascar Green requires a high degree of skill. It isn't something anyone can do with a grindstone and patience."

She shook her head briskly as though trying to wake up.

"Last week," I said, "you told me the Madagascar Green couldn't be peddled on the world market. But in the hands of a revolutionary group it could be used as a pledge for raising funds. Somehow, though, that possibility seems remote to me, so I'll guess it's in the hands of someone who intends to re-cut it, alter its appearance so that it can be sold or make two stones from it. The latter would offer the peddler the most security, but also the least profit. For all we know it's being cut and polished right now—or on its way to Amsterdam in the heel of a smuggler's shoe."

She looked numb.

"Maybe you would have preferred not knowing, but last week you seemed to have a large interest in the emerald and I thought you might want to follow through."

She nodded slowly and stiffly, like an animated doll. "At least you didn't tell Father."

"If he has to send the stone back to his country the fraud will be noticed, Iris. It can be detected as quickly as I found it."

Her eyes lifted and there was pleading in them. "Steve, tell me what to do."

CHAPTER ELEVEN

Picking up her empty glass, I mixed another gin and tonic and carried it back to her. "In times of stress," I remarked, "a dram or two of hard stuff doesn't hurt. I hate to be a bearer of bad tidings, but on the positive side I have an idea we might kick around. On several occasions I have mentioned the name of Artie Von Amond to various members of your family. A week ago, for fifty dollars, he located Silvio Contreras for you. Silvio was dead when found, but that wasn't Artie's fault. After all, we didn't specify that he bring him back alive."

She nibbled the drink a little and stared at it vacantly. "You want me to hire him?"

"To find the Madagascar Green. He gets retainers from several insurance companies for just that sort of thing. The stone wasn't insured, so that makes it a special case for him—I may have mentioned that Artie gets a hundred dollars a day plus expenses. I remember telling your father that the fee buys the time, skill, and resources of a number of people, to whom acquiring news of stolen gems is part of their routine. This case will be harder, because I don't expect the thief to call Artie and offer to sell it back. That's what usually happens and from then on it's just a question of price. And the Madagascar Green isn't some thousand-dollar diamond a thief might try to fence, so that cuts off a usual and important source of information. What it boils down to is looking for a unique stone too valuable to sell, one which will be kept hidden until it can be re-cut. It won't be easy to find."

She stubbed out her cigarette. "Very well, I'll hire him. Because I know you're unwilling to look for it anymore, and I hardly blame you. A week ago I had no idea that Silvio would be found dead."

"Well, we know one thing now that we didn't know then. Because Silvio couldn't have mailed the doublet to your father yesterday I think we can assume whoever did was the one who lifted the Madagascar Green from Silvio. So he's the man we want. And there's the jeweler who copied the doublet from the real stone. That's two men to look for. For Artie it should be helpful."

The door buzzer rang and Iris got up from the sofa, crossed to the door, and opened it. A man was standing outside. He wore a gray summer-weight suit and a Panama hat.

Iris said, "Oh—Lieutenant Kellaway."

"Yes, ma'am. Could you spare a moment?"

"Why, yes." She stepped back and Lieutenant Kellaway came in.

She said, "This is Mr. Bentley, Lieutenant. We were just having a gin and tonic. Would you join us?"

I got up and shook hands with the detective. He wiped his forehead and said, "It sure sounds good, but I'd better not. I have to get back to headquarters and the chief would sort of resent a heavy breath."

To me Iris said, "The lieutenant came here the other evening. In connection with what happened next door."

Kellaway looked at me. He was a heavy-faced man with thick, black eyebrows and a heavy beard. What had grown out since morning showed white bristles among the black and it looked rugged enough to rasp concrete. He said, "You knew Farnham?"

"I met him once," I said.

Kellaway shrugged. "A lot of people knew the dead man, but nobody's come forward and admitted having cut his throat. We haven't arrested anyone yet, but then we didn't have much to go on." He jabbed his hand into his right coat pocket. "Mrs. Sewall," he said apologetically, "I hate to break in on you like this, but we found something yesterday up in Montrose Park that may have a bearing on the murder." His hand pulled out something and when he opened his palm a knife handle was lying on it. Only it wasn't just a knife handle. It was a switchblade knife, the blade still sunk inside the haft. He slid the switch and the blade shot out. It was six or seven inches long, a thin blade that tapered to a fish-knife point. There were spots of rust on the blade.

"Some kids playing up in the park came across this lying near the fence that separates the park from the cemetery." He turned the knife over and pointed to a chip in the bone handle. "We think someone walking in Montrose Park heaved the closed knife toward the tall grass of the old cemetery, but the knife hit one of the iron fence palings and bounced back. The cemetery's locked at night, you know, so whoever it was couldn't have got inside to dispose of the knife. And in the darkness, if he heard the knife hit the fence, he wouldn't have been able to find it to throw again. That's what we figure, anyhow."

Placing the knife on the chow table, he straightened and said, "Despite the weathering and the kids digging sand with it there were still traces of blood around the base of the blade. Enough so the lab men could classify the blood type. It was human blood, Mrs. Sewall, and it corresponds to Mr. Farnham's blood type. That doesn't mean he was necessarily killed by this knife, but it could have been the weapon. And Montrose Park is only about four blocks from here—up on R Street."

Iris said, "If you're going to ask me if I've ever seen the knife before, I haven't. Actually it's the first one like it I've ever seen."

Kellaway sighed heavily and grimaced. "I had to ask," he said, and picked up the knife. "Part of the routine. In most states a switchblade's illegal, but they still bring them in from Mexico and Italy. Hell of a thing for kids to be playing with. They'd have it yet if the park patrolman hadn't happened to notice them on the sandpile. Well, much obliged, Mrs. Sewall. Sorry I had to trouble you."

"Quite all right, Lieutenant," she said pleasantly and walked toward the door to see him out. Kellaway looked around at me, and said, "You live in Georgetown?"

"No," I told him, "I work for a living."

That seemed to please him, and he began walking toward Iris. He stopped beside the dwarf tree, and said, "Bonsai. Very pretty, too." He bent over it and gave it a close inspection. "Chinese Juniper," he murmured. "Around four hundred years old. Look at that thick bark!" Straightening, he said, "That's a rare one, all right. Hope you're taking good care of it, Mrs. Sewall. Liquid fertilizer, minerals, and all that?"

"One of the gardeners from the Japanese Embassy comes over to care for it. I don't know the first thing about it. But how do you happen to know so much about Japanese dwarf trees, Lieutenant?"

He sighed. "I was there during the Occupation—Army CID. When the wife came over she got interested in flower arranging and bonsai. In self-defense I took a course in it and started growing a few. Then I learned I couldn't take them back here so I gave it up. It would have been something for my old age—not having any children."

Iris said, "Please let me know if I can help you, Lieutenant."

"I will, ma'am," he said, as he went out of the door.

Iris closed it, glanced at the bonsai, and shook her head. Then she came back to the sofa.

"You never know," I remarked.

"Never. But that dreadful knife. Steve—it was like having a ghost in the room."

"I'll make a little bet right now," I said. "I'll bet Tracy's murder is solved, and in the not-too-distant future."

"What makes you say that? The knife?"

"Sure. It's the first break in the case."

"I don't see why. There are thousands of knives just like it."

"Similar to it, perhaps, but that knife had belonged to someone for a long time. The cutting edge was beginning to recede from sharpening. The number and kind of men who carry switchblades is limited, and the number of men who keep that kind of knife long enough to wear away the blade by honing is even more limited. See what I mean?"

"You seem to know a great deal about criminal subjects."

"Picked it up in Leavenworth. Five years for tax evasion."

She shook her head and smiled slightly. "Shall we become serious again?"

"By all means. I'll call Artie and tell him to start working."

"If you must," she said and her voice sounded tired and hopeless.

"Believe me," I said, "Artie or someone like him should have been called the moment your father discovered the emerald was missing. As it is, valuable time has been lost, the waters are muddier than a horse pond, and the thief has an excellent chance of getting away clean. I know you hadn't seen much of Silvio in the last couple of years, but Artie will want to know about anyone Silvio saw on his trips here. He probably didn't have many friends in Washington, so checking them shouldn't be too hard. Artie will want their names and anything else you know about them."

"Very well, I'll make a list."

"Put your heart into it," I said. "The sooner Artie finds the Madagascar Green the sooner you can stop paying a hundred a day."

"Yes."

"I take it Sara isn't to know any of this?"

"Why should she?"

"Because she knew Silvio. She snared his heart, didn't she? Well, she might know something of his habits, his acquaintances. Enough to point to someone."

Her lips set. "Sara isn't to know. She's not—well, the responsibility's mine. Since Mother died I've done what I could to look after her, protect her."

"That's up to you, of course, but if you try to buck Artie you're only cheating yourself." I lowered my empty glass to the chow table, squared my shoulders, and said, "That sort of leaves everything in your hands, Iris—where they belong. I'll call Artie for you. If you want, I'll brief him on what's happened. That ought to save you for the kind of thoughtful answers he'll want to his questions on Silvio's past."

"That would be kind of you," she murmured. "Please do."

"Well," I said, "I'm on my way. Artie will want to see you later."

"Where are you going?"

"Down to the Yacht Club," I told her. "It's a halfway place to meet Artie, and with luck I'll be able to get an early start down the river."

Her eyes regarded me languidly. "How far are you going?"

"Well, I might make it as far as Quantico tonight."

"I've done a lot of sailing. I don't suppose I could persuade you to carry a working crew?"

"Honey," I said, "having you on board would be like tossing matches in the gas tank."

She shrugged. "A compliment, I suppose."

"It is," I said, "in its way. Oh, one other thing. Even the police haven't suggested any connection yet between the two murders. The only place they brush at all is your uncle's shop—Tracy owned part of the business. Now I'm not suggesting a positive link, but without skulking about in dark alleys maybe I could get a question answered."

"Go ahead."

"You've been in The Fiesta Shop, Iris. Are there any grinding wheels there? Any kind of stone-cutting or polishing equipment? It wouldn't have to be much."

She shook her head. "Uncle Oscar's too clumsy to be any sort of craftsman. No, the shop's like any other shop of its kind. A display room and a stock room behind the partition. And no grinding wheels."

"Fair enough," I said. "Forget I mentioned it."

I opened the door and closed it behind me. On the lawn a flock of grackles had driven away the robins and were busy snatching up clover seed with their gunmetal beaks. When bums moved in the better class moved out.

On Wisconsin the first rush of traffic out to Virginia had tapered off and you could see separate cars instead of what looked like a Detroit assembly line, bumper-to-bumper. But in four or five hours they would be on their way back, the passengers sunburned and a little addled from ale and light wines. Saturday afternoon around Washington.

Walking down to Martin's, I turned in, went to the phone booth, and dialed Artie's number. It rang for a while and then the answering service cut in and took my message. Stepping out of the booth I sat at a small table and ordered draft beer and a small steak. When I'd finished, a cab took me over K Street to Rock Creek Parkway, past the Lincoln Memorial and past the Tidal Basin to Maine Avenue. At the Yacht Club I went into the locker room, changed my clothes, and had a drink sent down.

Several drinks later Artie arrived. He looked hot and a little breathless. I waited until the waiter brought him a drink and then we walked out onto the pier. We sat in a corner shadowed from the sun and he said, "It must be a dirty job, Steve, or we could have handled it with a call. Instead, you put me on rush notice, break me away from the ball game, and we sidle off to a quiet corner where nobody can hear us talking. Am I right?"

I nodded.

"Okay, what is it?"

"The same dirty job we started last week, Artie. Only there were things you didn't know about it then."

For the next fifteen minutes I told him. He asked a few questions but he let me tell it my way. When I finished he stared at the bottom of his empty glass. His face had all the emotion of an unbaked pie crust. Finally he blinked and said, "A real honey.

I'm supposed to fetch back a million-dollar emerald without letting anyone know it's missing in the first place."

"That's about it."

"Discretion, you tell me. How the hell can you be discreet looking for a million dollars?"

"Well," I said, "far be it from me to tell you your business, but I'd run the Silvio thing down as far as it goes—you might pick up some interest there. Then the question of who made the doublet has to be answered. Through the police you ought to be able to find out if there are any shady jewelers in town—not just the kind who sell ten-buck watches and greeting cards, but fences who have a record of altering stolen stones on their own. The one we're looking for would be pretty skillful. Someone from the Old World, possibly, and probably an old lag. When you get the list I'd like to look it over."

His eyes looked out over the water and his voice was bitter. "I suppose you're going to get into that boat of yours now and sail off somewhere."

"I didn't put on dirty dungarees just to mow the lawn. Anything else?"

"That's enough," he said sourly. "You and your fancy friends. Have a ripping time."

He set the glass on the pier, stood up, and lumbered away.

I watched him go, shouldered a case of beer, and rowed it out to the ketch. Casting off, I upped sail and steered slowly out into the channel. There was barely enough wind to lift a feather, but as I tacked along toward Hains Point I told myself it was smart to relax while I could. The water was a silver mirror and after a while what wind there was fell off and I never got any farther than Bolling Field. The auxiliary wouldn't start and repairing it would have meant working up a heavy sweat, so I ran up the Becalmed signal and about four o'clock a proud-looking cruiser took pity on me and towed me back to the buoy.

CHAPTER TWELVE

The movie was Marlon Brando with gauze tapes slanting his eyelids and a straw coolie hat shaped like a hollow gong, the kind J. Arthur Rank's blacksmith beats in those British films. In the picture Brando spoke a lot of Japanese and some English. The pronunciation of both was bad, but I assumed there was artistry behind it all.

I walked down to the Occidental, ate Wiener Schnitzel, and drank a bottle of Guinness. Nothing seemed doing, so I left and took a taxi up Massachusetts to my apartment.

The TV program featured dance bands around the country: Les Brown, Ray Anthony, and Buddy Morrow. For some reason the producers had neglected "Whoopee John" Wilfahrt's old-time combo, a big favorite around St. Paul. Well, maybe next week.

My bookshelves were filled with tomes I had bought and promised myself to read, feeling that a man's education shouldn't end with a college diploma. I got as far as taking one down and reading the author's blurb. A very tony, intellectual-type gentleman indeed, and I felt sure his message held much for me. However, I begged off on grounds of eye-strain and returned $3.95 of paper and buckram to the shelf. Maybe someday.

There was work at the office, of course, but I'd been there once today and it meant a trip back downtown. The few girls I knew would be out on the town by now, and most of the sober CPA's had wives and families to attend to. All of which threw

me back on my own resources. How limited they were began
to emerge.

I built a drink for myself, changed TV channels, and began
watching a detective story. One man, presumably the heavy, was
slapping around a blonde and trying to tamper with her clothes.
Another man, her husband perhaps, was trying to prevent it, and
so there were blows.

I watched the tale unfold until, a little later, the camera
lingered too long on a sequence and one corpse got up and
walked away. After that I clicked off the set and sat back gritting
my teeth and drumming my fingers on the chair.

The phone rang and I got up gratefully to answer it. I heard
Artie's gravel voice saying, "Steve, what the hell you doing home?
I thought you'd be halfway to Norfolk by now."

"Read The Ancient Mariner," I said. "The part where the
wind stops blowing for days at a time."

"Buy a porpoise," he said and laughed. "Say, that's pretty
funny, isn't it? You know, like the old cry, 'Buy a horse.'"

"You want to lay off the stuff, Artie," I told him, "when you're
working."

"Hell, I can only afford it when I'm working."

"You're in a fine, silly humor, so it must be you've turned up
the stone and all's well."

"Not so quick," he complained. "I put in a little time doing
research at the Library. I got the stone's history and made a sketch
of it from a picture. Man, that's a lot of glass!"

"A real chunk. What else?"

"One of the lads did a rundown on the local jewelers like you
suggested. You'd be surprised how many learned their trades in
a striped suit."

"Maybe I wouldn't."

"Got your pencil ready?"

"Hold it." I went to the desk, brought back pencil and paper,
and said, "Shoot."

"There's a Dutchman named Groot over on Sixth Street who did a stretch back in the late thirties but he's been clean ever since. Almost blind now."

"Next."

"A refugee named Max Weiskold who got his training in Holland before the war. He's a known fence, one who co-operates with the police so they don't bother him. He runs a kind of hobby shop down on M Street."

"Okay."

"Pablo Sabatini's out on parole for diverting jeweler's gold and smuggling it to Cuba. Has a classy joint selling crystal and silverware out Columbia Road. Strings pearls and sets precious stones."

"Sounds good."

"Yeah. Sabatini. Where the hell have I heard that name before?"

"He wrote a screenplay for Tyrone Power, but that was years back. Next?"

"Well, an old con named Louie Arnold runs a combination loan shop and jewelry store down on D Street near Seventh. He's done two stretches for fencing and altering hot stones for resale. That does it, Steve. My man came up with eleven names altogether but those four are the most likely for the list."

"Why pad it with Groot? How the hell can a blind man cut precious stones?"

"How the hell can a blind guy play the piano?"

"Listen," I said, "TV's bad enough without every detective in town trying to sound like Joe Thursday. If I want laughs, there's always Baltimore."

"Yeah. Well, anything else?"

"Find the emerald," I said. "Find it fast."

"Just like that."

"Just like that."

The phone slammed down at the other end and I picked up my notes and carried them over to my desk. Flattening a street map, I took five thumbtacks and stuck them into the map. The first located Calvo's Embassy, the second the Hotel Flora where we had found Silvio, and the other three, the town addresses Artie had just given me. I stepped back and surveyed my work.

The thumbtack pattern showed Louie Arnold's establishment five blocks south of the Hotel Flora, the Embassy lay almost in the center of a two-mile line between Sabatini and Weiskold. If I had been hoping to find some extraordinary clue all I had learned was that Silvio had died five blocks from the jewelry store of a man who had served two terms in prison. Pulling out the tacks, I folded the map and put it away. Tomorrow, damn me, I knew I'd want to look in on the three jewelers.

I was picking up my drink when the door buzzer sounded. It cut through the quiet room like a klaxon, blared a second time, and I opened the door in self-defense.

The girl who stood there was wearing a white linen suit. Below her left shoulder was a flame-red brooch that matched her fingernails. Her right hand clasped a linen-covered purse. She had good legs and excellent ankles. She was Sara Cutler. Her fingers tapped the side of her purse and she said, "Hello, Steve. Surprised to see me?"

"Just a little."

She came in and I closed the door.

"It's a long drive from Warrenton," I said.

She nodded. "I seem to be commuting. Last night I drove Iris home."

"So I hear." I reached for my pipe, lighted it, and said, "I suppose I shouldn't have walked out on Iris last night but at the time it seemed like the thing to do."

She laughed a little. "It rather surprised her, you know. It isn't something that happens a lot."

"Probably not."

She blew smoke toward the TV screen and said, "I haven't been in a bachelor's apartment in a long time."

"Since when?" I asked. "Since last Sunday when Tracy was chauffeuring you through the rain? Then on Monday hot buttered rums and scones and a gambol beside the slate fireplace before he was killed?"

She was staring at her drink. After a while she said in a tight voice, "It wasn't what you think, Steve. Not at all. I never thought of Tracy that way."

"Just how did you think of him?"

Her eyes lifted and they had the odd diffuse quality of dusty pearls. "He wasn't my lover if that's what you meant."

"I see," I said. "He was just one of those unusually understanding fellows a girl can open her heart to. Would that be it?"

She shook her head and her lips were tight. "Please, Steve. He's dead. So let's not talk about him."

I eased myself into a chair facing her and said, "If it will make you feel any better the police have turned up a clue. A switchblade knife found up in Montrose Park. They think it could have done the job."

"Will they find the murderer?"

"Yes," I said, "I think they will. But whether they ever stumble across the reason for Silvio's death is another thing. That's because Farnham meant a little something in this town; he even died in the right place. That's a contrast to Silvio gasping his life away in a shabby room on a tick-infested mattress. Who cares about a junkie dead in Chinatown—a foreigner at that?"

She said nothing, but her face was taut.

"You knew Silvio—he was even in love with you. Did you know he was an addict?"

"I—I suspected it."

"You knew where he got the stuff?"

She shook her head.

"He must have known someone in Washington—he came here every month or so for several years."

"He spoke English badly. He'd have dinner with bachelors from the Embassy or Uncle Oscar. When you're alone in a foreign country you tend to stay with your own kind."

"Didn't he know anyone else?"

"If he did I've forgotten. Steve, he was only a courier—I never even went out with him. I couldn't help that he fell in love with me—he was a lonely boy. I didn't love him but I'm sorry about the way he died. Was that what you were seeing Father about this morning?"

"Who told you I was there? Iris?"

She shook her head. "Uncle Oscar. He saw you leave the embassy."

"He ought to stay behind the counter and push those Indian herbs and baskets," I said. "Or maybe he's out making high-level contacts while some other fellow runs the store."

"You don't like Uncle Oscar?"

"I'm like Switzerland—neutral about the whole thing."

"Don't think badly of him, Steve. He's doing as well as he can. And he's proud of my father, not envious of him."

"Why not? I am. So's anybody else with the ability to make comparisons."

The conversation was flagging, so was my drink.

She looked at me for what seemed like a long time, and then she said, "Steve, don't you know why I'm here?"

"Not unless you want another palm reading."

"Hardly that. No, it's because of Wayne."

It jarred me a little. I said, "What's he done now?"

"It seems he's managed to raise some money in a very good business deal. He's never discussed his affairs with me, so I didn't ask for particulars this time either. Anyway, it's a wonderful thing, Steve, because it makes everything so much easier."

"How?" I asked.

"Why, leaving him," she said, half in surprise. "What else? You know I'm not in love with him, but how could I leave him when he'd lost everything else?"

I stared at her for a while, then I picked up my drink, sipped it, and put it down. "Little sister," I said, "you're about as inconsistent as a woman can be. Last Sunday I thought you wanted me to investigate Wayne so you could sink bailing hooks in him, rip away the living flesh, and rattle his bones. It doesn't jibe with what you've just said."

"You were looking at it one way, I was looking at it differently."

"Too bad we couldn't have got together," I said dryly. "Next time I run away from ten grand please slap my silly face. Well, now that I know your motives were pure, what do you intend to do?"

"Leave him," she said quietly. "He'll be better off without me."

"No one would."

"Is that just a manner of speaking?"

"I suppose so."

"You wouldn't be in love with me, would you?"

"It's possible."

"Only you don't want to be, is that it?"

I shrugged. "It wouldn't work out. Not for me and certainly not for you."

Her head tilted a little. "The gamble wouldn't appeal to you?"

"Angel," I said, "two bucks across the board at Bowie is the height of folly for me. Last night I got a little carried away by everything—the thin expensive air we were breathing, I guess— but some hours later when I got a grip on myself again I realized that all your life you've had guys like me pawing the air when you pass. I come from a simple, ordinary sort of world. I don't know any politicians or diplomats or financiers; except for the war I haven't traveled anywhere, and certainly not to the fashionable spas. I'm not of the landed gentry and when I tried to ride a Shetland pony at age nine I fell off. I wouldn't know a Hereford from a Black Angus or a Riley from a Daimler. I don't summer at the Shore and winter on Hog Island. I couldn't board a wife on Foxhall Road or in a Mayflower suite; the maximum I can hope for is a three-bedroom rambler out in the Bell Haven with a high fence for the kids. There'd be no French chef, no upstairs maid, no governess, and no laundress. For years we'd have to hide money like pack rats just to see the children through school. You wouldn't necessarily know it, but that's the way most of America lives. I'll concede you the best intentions in the world, angel, but it isn't the kind of life you were born to, and it certainly isn't the sort you've always known. The fact that you'd even consider me goes a long way toward making this a spectacular summer for me, but in short it wouldn't work out."

She said tightly, "Is there anything else?"

"No."

"You've said everything you wanted to?"

"Yes."

"Then let me say this: I thought you were a special sort of man and I still do. Unfortunately you paint yourself as a simple homespun character with middle-class goals, and there's nothing wrong with that, except that it's a calculated deception. You're alert, quick, and highly intelligent. You've proved yourself in the world of business and you have your clients' respect. By any standards you're quite sufficiently cultured to mingle with any social group. You're honest, solid, and you have integrity. And beneath it all you're a little bit of a snob. Do I make myself clear?"

I laughed shortly. "A snob?"

She nodded. "It works both ways. And for a man as perceptive as you it's apparently never occurred to you that the kind of life you've described is the kind I might always have wanted. You hate sham and phoniness don't you? Well, so do I. It's what I hate most in life—the deceits and pretentions we're all guilty of just to live smoothly and get what we want. I wish life were different but it isn't. I hoped you might have seen a vision of going through life with me, but apparently that calls for too much imagination. But I can see it, Steve. I can see it clearly, and that's what I want."

"It wouldn't work. You know it and so do I."

"All right—suppose it didn't. We'd have some happiness, wouldn't we? Some years together—some wonderful months at the least. For the kind of world we live in, isn't that worth taking?"

There were tears in her eyes. I took her hand and pulled her down beside me. Her shoulders began to shake and muffled sobs came and after a while I took out a handkerchief and gave it to her. She calmed down then, turned to me, and said, "If you were trying to humiliate me you couldn't have done a better job."

"Now who's talking about pride?" I asked.

"You haven't answered me," she said levelly.

"Because there isn't any pat answer. For one thing you hardly know me. I can be selfish, short, and inconsiderate and I probably drink too much. I'm self-centered and set in my ways. I'm not even particularly ambitious. These are things you don't know about me but in marriage they're awfully important. You came here tonight in an emotionally disturbed state because you were leaving your husband. That's a big decision to make, but you got over the hurdle. It's only natural to look to someone else for affection and understanding now, and in my case I've got some to spare. But I think we'd do well to wait until you're free from Wayne before we talk about it again."

Her lips were brushing the side of my cheek. She whispered, "That's fair." Then she turned her face and our lips met. Hers were warm and sweet and soft. She murmured, "I thought you might have wanted Iris."

I shook my head. "Not Iris. You."

Sitting up, she tucked my handkerchief back into my pocket. "This afternoon I moved into an apartment—the Belgrave over on Connecticut. It's not far, you know. Will you remember it?"

"Like the date of the Norman Conquest."

I got up. She lighted a cigarette and was gazing at the ceiling. "Two divorces in the family," she said. "Father will lose his mind."

"He has other problems," I said. "He'll hardly notice it."

"What kind of problems?"

"Oh, unrest back home. Political uncertainty. The kind of thing that gives ambassadors gray hair and lined faces."

"It's always been that way. As long as I can remember. You're sure it isn't something else?"

"Positive," I lied.

The telephone rang and when I answered it was Iris. Her voice sounded querulous as she said, "Steve, Mr. Von Amond has just left here, and I must say I find him very unimpressive. Do you really think he can find the emerald?"

"He can give a good professional try," I said. "Smarten up and don't rate a man by the kind of collar he wears. He's selling you a quarter-century of experience in just this kind of thing. They don't come any abler."

"Well," she pouted, "that's somewhat reassuring, but so far as I can see he hasn't done a thing yet. Not one solitary thing. I wish you hadn't walked out entirely."

"Maybe I haven't" I said, "but if I get any ideas I'll tell Artie."

There was a pause. "You're frightfully busy, I suppose?"

"You could put it that way."

"Too busy to drop over and hear a little hi-fi with me?"

"Much too busy," I said. "This has turned out to be the busiest night of the year. People all over the place."

"Kindly go to hell then," she said irritably, and hung up.

Sara said, "A client?"

"In a way."

"I suppose clients can be very inconsiderate."

"They can indeed, but it's a living. I have the kind of open, honest face people bring problems to."

"I know," she said reflectively, and blew smoke toward the air-conditioner. "You have yourself under perfect control at all times. I'm here in your apartment, having practically proposed to you, and you haven't even made a man-sized pass at me. Little good it's done me to come here at all."

"I'm all tied up in middle-class scruples," I said. "Not playing house with another man's wife just about heads the list. If it makes me dull company, why, there's always Paul Sewall."

"As if I didn't know." She shivered a little. "Frankly, I'd be grateful for a little gaiety this evening. Could I persuade you to be seen with me at the Bagatelle?"

"Easily." I pulled her to her feet.

"You have been in nightclubs before?" she teased.

"Not since I was young and foolish."

"Think you can remember how it used to be?"

"I'll stagger through it," I told her. "Come what may."

CHAPTER THIRTEEN

The bagatelle was half a block off Connecticut, not far from the Mayflower, in the district where a foot of frontage equals a bar of gold at Fort Knox. The building was an old one. It had been built as a town mansion, turned into a rooming house during Prohibition, and since then it had sheltered a number of night clubs, all with different names and backers, but with the same general approach to life. According to gossip, the man who bankrolled the Bagatelle was Vance Bodine.

The façade was a lot of glass brick, glowing with subdued violet light. The handrail up the five marble steps was twisted wrought iron, and the uniformed doorman wore an Astrakhan busby three inches taller than that of the Coldstream Guards. Take away the fancy dress and he was a thin-faced monkey with cold eyes and cruel lips. When he looked at me they seemed to sneer, but when he saw Sara he bowed so low I thought the busby might tumble off.

He opened the oak door and the checkroom girl hurried to the doorway to reach for a hat I didn't have. The captain of waiters wore an indigo frock coat with silver epaulettes and thick silver braid along the trouser seam. He bowed to Sara, said, "Good evening, Mrs. Cutler," and led us to a table beside the dance floor.

The walls were scalloped with crescent booths of cream-colored leather. In a corner was a service bar with no bar stools, a device to discourage table-hoppers. Overhead a velvet sky was dotted with small silver dice that looked, at first, like stars. There was barely enough light to read the printing on the silver-dusted

menus the captain placed on the table. On a small raised dais
stood four or five music stands, and in front of it, partly on the
dance floor, a grand piano. Even with the piano there was plenty
of space for three couples to dance. The place looked about three-
quarters full. Not rush business for Saturday night, but there
were no major conventions in town. The crowd included the
usual gathering of five-percenters, customers' men, and New
York bankers with their fancy women.

Sara said, "I'm not at all hungry, Steve. Suppose we just have
a drink?"

"Two Scotch," I told the captain of waiters. "The soda
separate."

The orchestra was filing in, butting cigarettes and getting
ready to play. Vibes, drums, tenor sax, muted trumpet, and an
accordion.

Except for the drummer the sidemen stood behind the music
stands when they began to play. It was quiet, unobtrusive music,
with just enough lift to be danceable. Imitation Buddy De Franco.
Our drinks came and the waiter mixed them for us, hovered a
moment, and glided away as softly as a snake on velvet.

We danced and it was easier than leading a rag doll, no
resistance at all; anticipation, if anything. Her head was on my
shoulder, her eyes half-closed, and it came to me that I had not
danced in a long while; probably never with so beautiful a girl.
When the floor got crowded we went back to the table and ordered
another drink. The set was ending, anyway, and when the floor
was clear a man in an indigo dinner jacket stepped in front of the
dais and a thin microphone slid down from the ceiling. He said,
"Good evening, ladies and gentlemen. The Bagatelle takes great
pleasure in introducing that sensational entertainer, appearing
exclusively at the Bagatelle for your entertainment pleasure—
Miss Janice Western!"

He sprinted away from the microphone, and from behind
the dais came Miss Janice Western. She was wearing a red net

dress, an orchid corsage on the left shoulder strap, and she bowed to scattered applause. A waiter was at the piano, holding a chair for her, and she sat down, adjusted herself, and struck a chord. She hummed a brief introduction and began to sing I Get a Kick Out of You.

Turning from her, I looked at Sara. Her eyes were fixed on Janice Western, her face set in a hard mold, her hands motionless. Janice Western had a pleasant voice with a frayed, throaty quality, a little like Der Bingle in contralto. She played very little piano, just enough to give a minimum background for her voice. At the release the drummer joined in with light brush work and on the final chord the band filled in.

The crowd applauded and Janice Western smiled amiably, a little condescendingly. She had the look of a female with plenty in the bank and a private way to get more. To Sara I said, "This shows how much I get around. I had no idea Janice was in show business."

Her voice came from far away. "I wanted to see the woman who took away my husband." She turned to me. "I don't think much of Wayne's taste, do you?"

I shrugged. "She may have special talents. If she were more beautiful than you, you might have reason to blame yourself, but since she isn't you can blame Wayne. It's that simple."

"I suppose it is," she said without conviction. "She looks like a perfect bitch, doesn't she? A kept woman."

"Well, I said, "at least she's Bodine's kept woman now."

"There's that, I suppose." She gazed at her drink, picked up the glass, and finished it. Altogether quite a swallow.

Janice sang a second song and then another. The most you could say for them was that the enunciation was perfect; you could hear every word. And all the time Sara said nothing. Her face was a little flushed and her eyes stared at the top of the table. It was plain that things were going on in her mind, having mostly to do with the humiliation of losing a man to another woman. Even though it was a man she said she did not love.

When the third song ended Janice Western stood up, took several bows, and walked to the side of the dais. The spotlight lingered on her as she sat down at a table—long enough to show the face of the man she was joining. He was a big man with an olive skin, dressed in a wide-shouldered suit that gleamed like silk. His sleeve showed two inches of French cuff and from a high pinch collar a purple tie trailed down like spilled grape juice. Then the light was gone and I could barely see the two of them.

Sara said, "That man she's with—you know him?"

"He's Tip Cadena, one of Vance Bodine's chief bolos."

"The one you struck at Vance's party?"

"I didn't know you noticed."

"I watched from the bar. Remember?"

I sipped my drink and lighted a cigarette. "In the world of the gutter, Cadena holds a high position. He handles numbers collections mostly, and if there's any stalling he'll carve his initials on a man's arm just as a gentle reminder."

"You're not serious."

"Angel," I said, "the world isn't limited to fawning diplomats and wine-coated steeplechase riders. There's a lot of scum floating around the sewers of the world. That's where the Tip Cadenas thrive."

Just then a man's voice behind me said, "Hello, darling. Didn't take long to patch your broken heart, did it?" The words were slightly slurred and they held the harmonics of a sneer. I turned, glanced up, and saw Wayne Cutler.

His dark skin was pale under the eyes, his short black hair was slightly mussed, and as he stared back at me he teetered and gripped the back of my chair to keep from falling. Far from his best, he was still handsome. He grunted, peered at me again, and said, "Don't think I've met you. I've seen you before, though. At Bodine's. I suppose you're one of his stinking crowd."

Sara glanced at me, then at her husband. "Just go away, Wayne," she told him. "People are staring at us."

"They are, are they? Well, you shouldn't object. Not ever. That's what you live for, isn't it? Stares and admiration? From anyone who'll give it to you."

She turned away angrily. Cutler leaned forward and patted the top of my head. "I'm the injured husband," he confided. "Maybe Sara tells it different, but that's the way it is. If you don't believe me, wait till the divorce brings it all out. Sara thinks I'm going to be a co-operative fool, but I'm not. I'll show her up for what she is."

"Wayne!" Sara snapped.

He stepped back, smiled a drunk's foolish smile, and staggered away.

Sara said, "Thanks, Steve. For not hitting him. A scene like that would be more than I could stand."

"It's time we left, anyway."

She nodded, reached into her purse, and began to touch up her lips.

Out of the corner of my eye I saw Wayne Cutler making his uncertain way toward the end table where Janice Western was sitting with Tip Cadena. Reaching it, he leaned forward and placed his palms on the table and said something to Janice Western. She turned away from him. Cadena said something to Cutler, who answered him, and then their voices rose. Cadena was half out of his chair when Cutler swung at him. The blow glanced off Cadena's shoulder, and then Cadena's fist jabbed out. It was a short punch, no more than six inches, but it landed just above Cutler's belt. As he doubled over, Cadena's hand chopped down on the back of his neck. Cutler went the rest of the way down, his hand spilling a drink. Janice Western, got up quickly and disappeared behind the bandstand.

Two waiters rushed over and got Cutler to his feet but his head hung forward like a pumpkin on a string. Between them they hustled him out of a side doorway.

Sara's face was white. She wet her lips and said huskily, "I've got to help him, Steve. I can't let them hurt him anymore."

I nodded, signaled the waiter, and paid the check. Fifteen dollars. Fifteen dollars for what? I asked myself as we went out of the side exit where the waiters had taken Wayne Cutler.

Outside was the Bagatelle parking lot. The waiters were pushing Cutler's limp body into the back seat of a Cadillac convertible. The top was down and I could see a man getting behind the wheel. Sara said, "That's Wayne's car."

"Is that his chauffeur?"

"No. He drives it himself."

"Well," I said, "it looks as if the Bagatelle has a well-rehearsed routine for taking care of objectionable guests. In this case your husband was asking for it."

She turned to me and her face was taut with worry. "Steve, I want him in my apartment."

I nodded, feeling my stomach turn cold, and walked past the lines of gleaming cars to the side of the Cadillac. Wayne Cutler's body was propped against the far corner of the rear seat and his eyes were closed. For all I knew Cadena's bolo punch had killed him.

The man behind the wheel had a dove-gray felt hat pulled low over his forehead. From between his lips grew a reedy brown cigarette. His cheeks were slightly sunken. The sound of his breathing was rasping and brittle, like the rustle of dry snakeskin.

I said, "Thanks, neighbor, but we'll see Mr. Cutler home."

"You said what?" The cigarette bobbed like a stumpy fishing pole. He was a young man, still in his twenties, but his voice was old.

I said, "We won't debate it. He's the lady's husband and she's taking over."

"I got orders," he told me. "Don't go buyin' yourself unnecessary trouble."

From his right pocket he took out a gun, laid his wrist on the edge of the door, and pointed the gun at me. "Get the idea?"

"Oh, sure," I said, "sorry and all that." I half-turned, my hand came up hard and slapped the gun away. I grabbed his wrist and leaned on it, grinding the bone into the partly raised window edge. He howled with pain and cursed me. I slapped his face and twisted his wrist. I put my shoulders into it and dragged him over the door, clawing and yelping. He lit on his knees, hard. He howled again and tried to bite my hand but I slammed my right knee against the side of his face and he toppled sideways and hit the macadam. He had lost all interest in the argument.

Sara was around on the other side of the car, stroking Wayne's forehead. She seemed to be crying a little. I watched for a moment, feeling a little sick, and then one of the waiters came over and picked up the forgotten pistol. He brought it to me and said, "You gonna give it back to him?"

I looked at it. A cheap Czech automatic, about 9 millimeter. "I'll keep it," I told him. "Around here I can see it coming in handy."

He shrugged, and began picking its owner off the asphalt.

Sara looked up from her husband. She said, "Is he hurt badly, Steve?"

I shook my head. "As it turns out I was tonight's only casualty."

I opened the door for her and she got behind the wheel and started the engine. "Take him home, angel," I said. "All the way. I guess you know he needs you. If only to keep the bottles out of reach."

She nodded slowly, bit her lip, and brushed away a strand of hair. Unevenly, she said, "Will you call me tomorrow?"

"No."

"Steve—what can I say?"

"Just don't say anything. It's one of those rare times when everyone understands words are unnecessary."

I stepped back from the side of the car and it pulled ahead and out of the parking lot, bouncing a little as its front wheels met the street. The tail lights were huge round rubies in the darkness.

Turning, I saw a man coming toward me. A big man with a straw hat and a purple tie. A yard from me he stopped, rubbed his fingers in the palm of his hand, and said, "You get around, Bentley. What's this about Giuseppe?"

"Cokie Joe?" I asked. "He pulled a prop gun on me but nobody laughed. He's backstage revising the act."

Cadena gave a short laugh. "The kid's excitable," he said. "A good kid but he shouldn't of done that. Hell, he was only doing a favor for a drunk."

"Mrs. Cutler had other ideas, but he got boorish."

"You making a big thing out of it?"

"Act your age. I was a victim of circumstances."

He took out a gold cigarette case, lighted a cigarette, and put the case away. The arc lights above gave his face a sallow color. He blew smoke over one shoulder, turned back to me, and said, "I figure you and Cutler don't get along too well."

"That's a good guess."

"Lucky for you," he remarked. "Vance don't exactly like guys who've handled his merchandise. Or their friends."

"Merchandise?" I said. "Like expensive women, or expensive jewels, or—"

He extracted the cigarette from his mouth and stared at me. Finally, he said, "I think you better shut up, Bentley."

"All finished with the heavy menace?" I asked. "Can I crawl away now for a small beer?"

"Good night, friend. Have yourself a bundle of sweet dreams."

"I'll try hard," I said, "after I get rid of the nightmares."

Cadena walked stiffly toward a sky-blue Chrysler. He got inside, closed the door, and growled the engine. The heavy car slid out of the parking lot like a yacht being launched. As I watched it vanish I saw a small black sedan pull away from the curb. It had dimmed headlights and it looked like a police car but I could have been wrong. Would a police car be tailing a criminal with as much influence behind him as Tip Cadena?

I handed my ticket to an attendant, paid him a dollar-fifty for the privilege, and when he brought around my Olds he squealed the brakes, getting back at me for neglecting the tip.

The way I was feeling it wouldn't do me any good to go back to my apartment. A few more drinks sitting up there alone and I'd gnaw my way through the woodwork. The door of Paradise had opened part way for me but the moment I turned my back it had closed again with a loud slam. Well, it was better to find out those things early than late. Much better. I had told her it would never work and for a while she had disbelieved me. It had taken her husband to show her I was right. Except for Paul Sewall, he had it made.

My face was cold, my lips numb and hard as frozen wax. A light wind was blowing up Connecticut. It might be enough to push the ketch but not as far as I wanted to go. For that I would need a hurricane.

Turning down Connecticut, I drove to the Yacht Club, changed clothes for the second time that day, and rowed out to the ketch. At first I couldn't get the running lights going, then I found the trouble and cast off. The wind was stronger than I had hoped. It blew from the port quarter with slow, steady force. Under the moon the river looked like black oil.

I broke out a can of beer and tried to drink it but it tasted warm and cottony and I dropped it overboard. The wake was opalescent in the moonlight. The green channel lights were emerald eyes staring at me out of the darkness. Off Hains Point I glanced at the chronometer and saw that it was a little after eleven o'clock. Just twelve hours since I had called on Ambassador Calvo and learned his emerald was a fraud.

The quiet whisper of the bow cutting water lulled me and relaxed my mind. I found another can of beer and this one tasted a little better. I got out my pipe and sat back smoking, my hand on the tiller, and after a while the lights of Alexandria came into view.

In a way, I guess I'd been trying to get a rise out of Cadena when I mentioned expensive jewels. It had occurred to me more than once that his interest—and Sewall's and Bodine's—in my activities might have been for reasons other than those they claimed. And if the reasons were the Madagascar Green, it seemed better to know it once and for all. At least that way I'd have a pretty definite idea what to expect from them. As things stood, though, I still didn't really know. But if I was right, it meant I'd soon get some special attention. How soon it would come was anybody's guess, and there was no second prize.

I thought about it for a long time—too long to do myself any good—and by two o'clock the ketch was drifting somewhere off Fort Washington. I lowered the sails, dropped anchor in deep water, and turned in.

CHAPTER FOURTEEN

Monday was as hot as the Monday before. A local beer shortage had developed and kids begged chips of ice from trucks delivering over on the East side. Outside it was too hot for coats or ties and people staggered from one air-conditioned building to another, swearing at the heat. But over on the Virginia shore where Potomac breezes cooled the big estates, the swimming pools were no busier than usual.

Around lunch time Mrs. Bross came into my office, panic on her face. "Mr. Bentley," she stammered, "there's … there's a … a policeman to see you."

"We always take two tickets to the Benefit," I said. "You know that."

"Mr. Bentley," she said, trying again, "he isn't selling anything. He just wants to see you."

I laid down my work. "Did you think to get his name?"

"Kellaway," she blurted unhappily. "Detective Lieutenant Kellaway. Oh, my."

"I'll see him," I said.

She heaved a great sigh, tottered away, and opened the door.

Kellaway came in. He looked grateful to be inside a cool office. I stood up and we shook hands. He sat down and said, "Sorry to take the time of a busy man, Mr. Bentley, but a thing or so has come up you might be able to shed some light on."

I sat back and blinked to ease my tired eyes. "Such as?"

"Well," he said, "just this. After meeting you the other day at Mrs. Sewall's place, I gave you a quick rundown—routine.

According to Police records you average about two tickets a year, one for speeding on Rock Creek Parkway, the other for parking overtime. So far as we know you've never passed any bad checks, gotten disorderly to the public dismay, or slugged a pay phone. In short, you're cleaner than a tout's pocket on Saturday night."

"Lieutenant," I said, "I'm probably one of the nicest and most law-abiding fellows you'll ever know. I've never even been pulled in on a stag-show raid. Alongside me, Li'l Abner is a convicted felon."

He smiled a little. A tired smile from a man whose face wasn't accustomed to it. "That's what makes it look odd—you knowing Tip Cadena."

I reached forward, took a pipe from the rack, filled and lighted it. When it was going well, I said, "This comes as something of a surprise. Just how would you know I even know the name?"

"For one thing you were seen in conversation with him last night. In the Bagatelle parking lot."

"So it was a police Chevvie after all," I mused. "Yes, we exchanged some words. You may also have heard I roughed up one of his monkeys named Giuseppe."

"I heard that, too. That what you were talking about?"

"Almost exclusively."

He shrugged his shoulders disappointedly. "So much for that."

I took the bit from between my teeth, cradled the pipe in my palms, and said, "Lieutenant, if you'd be a little less oblique we might travel faster and get further. If you're seriously interested in putting Tip Cadena behind bars, I'm a willing helper."

"Why?" he asked softly.

"It's a dirty town," I told him. "I don't like hoodlums, racketeers, dope peddlers, or numbers men who drain off a working man's pay envelope. For all I know there may be others like me. If so, our voices are small, smothered under the payoffs."

His mouth had drawn into a hostile line. I said, "I know you hate to hear an outsider criticize the Force, but any child of twelve knows what goes on. I don't like Cadena and I don't like the man behind him any better. Vance Bodine."

"Softly," he said, half-turning. "Whisper that name."

"Let's get down to cases. You've got a tail on Cadena, you're interested in him, and you're Homicide. The only other time I saw you, you were asking questions about a switchblade knife that may have killed Tracy Farnham, so I judge you'd like to link the knife to Tip. How right am I?"

"Close enough to win the day's parlay," he said quietly. "A stoolie claims the knife was Tip's, but we'd never get him to testify in court. At best, the lead is only circumstantial, so what we need is something resembling a motive. Cadena ties into Mrs. Sewall through her husband and Vance Bodine, whose lawyer Sewall is. The question, though, is how would Cadena tie into Tracy Farnham?"

I put my pipe back between my teeth, sucked on it a while, and said, "You're probably thinking Sewall might have fingered Farnham for making too free with his wife, but as I get it, Sewall didn't really care. For one thing, they're getting a divorce—or were at the last telling."

"Well, we don't put it down to a lover's quarrel. Usually that sort of thing is done on the spur of the moment by a killer who runs outside and into the arms of the first policeman to sob out the story. We're pretty sure no woman had the strength to slug him as hard as he was slugged before his throat was cut. So that leaves it at a man doing the job and the way the throat was cut it looked as though the killer had had some practice. You could see the vertebrae."

He looked at me. "Mrs. Sewall's prints were all over the apartment, as were those of her sister—Mrs. Cutler. Mrs. Cutler was with you at the Bagatelle, was she not?"

"I took her there," I admitted, "but she went home with her husband."

"Wayne Cutler," he said in a distant voice. "Think he might have done the job?"

"No," I said, "but that doesn't mean he didn't. Chances are he was down at the springhouse, locked inside with a cool stone jug. It would be easy enough to check. I'll say this much, though—Bodine wouldn't weep if you happened to settle on Cutler as the killer."

"Yeah," he said. "I wanted your impression. Some old Treasury hands seem to think you're a pretty smart lad."

"Mighty kind of them, but murder's a little out of my line. Tax frauds I can tell you about."

He grunted and stood up. "Thanks, Mr. Bentley. Sorry I took your time."

"No trouble," I said. "If I get any thoughts I'll let you know."

He nodded.

I said, "This is away from the main subject, but some ten days ago a corpse was found in a Chinatown flop called the Hotel Flora. According to the papers there was nothing unusual about the case. However, I understand the guy died of narcotic poisoning."

His eyes narrowed. "That wasn't in the papers, Mr. Bentley. How would you know that?"

"From Ambassador Calvo," I lied.

Kellaway folded his arms and looked at me. "What interests you? The narcotics angle?"

"Would an addict accustomed to measuring out crystals be likely to make a mistake and die of an overdose?"

Kellaway sat down again. "That's a pretty sharp question," he said. "Ask me another."

"Sure. Were the dead man's prints on the syringe?"

Kellaway's mouth twisted a little. "There were no prints at all."

I leaned back in my chair. "Why would a man who had just used a hypodermic syringe bother to wipe the barrel clean, Lieutenant? It seems like an unusual thing to do."

"Very unusual," he said. "We haven't answered that question yet, and if you're going to ask whether the case is closed, it isn't. We put out the story to soothe the killer's nerves."

"And the Ambassador's," I suggested.

"That, too."

He stood up again. "The Narcotics Squad's been looking into the guy's life a little, checking back over the last couple of years. It may mean nothing, but the boys seem to find a relationship between the times Contreras arrived in Washington and fresh drug supplies on the market."

"Was Cadena ever tied up with drug pushing?"

"He was tied up with everything," Kellaway said sourly, "but he was never booked for peddling. Figure he's a snowbird?"

I shook my head. "Bodine's too smart to have an addict working that close to him. Down the line, maybe, but Cadena's too close and he knows too much." I put down my pipe and got up. "If Contreras was murdered, Lieutenant, what was the motive?"

"There's been plenty of head-scratching over that one. The room had been torn apart so he must have hidden something. Drugs, maybe. Another junkie stole what he had. That's the present thinking."

I walked to the outer door with him, we shook hands, and I stretched and looked around the room. Mrs. Bross had left to claim her place in the cafeteria line. The office was as quiet and cool as an underground tomb, but across the street, from the tarred roof of a building, heat waves were rising like thin smoke from Indian campfires. Outside, the air would be blistering.

My coat was hanging on the rack but it looked hot and burdensome so I left it where it was, locked the office, and went down to the street.

It was too hot to walk to the Occidental so I slid into Walgreen's and ate a ham sandwich, standing because of the crowd. From there I got my Olds out of the garage and drove down to Seventh Street, parked near D, and walked the rest of the way.

Louie Arnold's place of business began half a floor above the street. Eight cast-iron steps from the time of Lincoln led up to the open doorway. Beneath them was an English basement with a weather-beaten sign on the door that said Private. The display window was gray with dust. Chipped paint letters spelled out Loans on Anything of Value. Another lettered sign read: Jeweler and Dealer in Old Gold. Behind the gray glass was an assortment of junk that looked like Great Grandmother's attic: a split-cane fishing rod with no reel, leaning against the side of the dirty window; a chest of drawers with peeling veneer and half the drawer knobs missing; a rusty Cavalry saber; a glass lamp mantel but no lamp; a typewriter that looked like one of the first made; a gramophone with a large flaring horn that lacked only a brown-and-white rat terrier with cocked ears; a green Civil War bugle with a bronze tassel also green; strings of colored glass beads; partial sets of china; a stuffed owl lacking one glass eye; a stuffed, motheaten gray squirrel mounted beside a stuffed chipmunk on a small birch log. And so on. Dust lay thick on everything. You could hardly read the inside sign: Taxidermy Done Here. A Notary Public notice would have brightened the place.

Inside, the jumble was even worse. The owner of these unclaimed treasures sat on an old four-legged stool, his cracked shoes resting on a dead, pot-bellied stove. I wasn't sure whether the stove was for sale too, or if it warmed the store. Louie Arnold held a wooden clothespin in his left hand. In his right hand was a small penknife with a worn blade. He was whittling his clothespin. Not carving anything out of it, just whittling. That made him a Yankee. I looked around for a cracker barrel, saw none, and decided it must have gone last winter in a shrewd antique deal.

He was a middle-aged man with a lined face, the two-day beard partly screening the lines. His upper hair was sparse and mostly gray. Hair stood out of his ears like a spray of ripe barley. The shirt he wore was yellowed and damp with sweat. The collar had been torn from it some years back. Stained gray suspenders were looped slackly over his shoulders. He opened his mouth to speak and I saw two gold teeth; the others were brown with nicotine.

"What'll ya have, mister?" he asked, without missing the stroke of his knife. "Milk china? Cut-glass bowls? Maybe some antique cherrywood? I got 'em all. You look like a feller who'd appreciate a real genuine antique."

"I would," I said, "and you've got 'em, only that's not for today. According to your sign you're a jeweler."

"Old gold, too. Buy or sell?"

"Neither one," I said. "As a matter of fact I was interested in something in the jewelry line. My girlfriend's got her heart set on a big good-looking stone for a ring. Topaz, maybe, or amethyst. Only I haven't got that kind of dough."

"What you got in mind?" he asked.

I shrugged. "Something that looks good for not much dough. It has to be big and flashy, but not expensive. Get the idea?"

"I got it."

"Fellow I know got a ring like that made up in Cincinnati a while back. Told me the jeweler took a thin slice of real stone and glued a synthetic piece on the bottom. Cost him a fraction of the real thing, and his wife—well, even she couldn't tell. My friend said the jeweler called it a doublet. Ever hear of a thing like that?"

The chips were still falling. Beside the stool the mound was an inch high. I said, "Could you make me a doublet?"

He hitched one of his suspenders and stared down at what was left of the clothespin. "I could once," he said morosely, "but I don't do that kind of work no more. Sold my wheel, cutting disks, and all the rest last year. To a young fellow just starting in. Told him I hoped it'd do better for him than it done for me."

"Much call for that sort of thing nowadays?" I asked.

"Doublets?" He shook his head. "Synthetics is what they all want now. Harder than the real thing and cheaper. Not many people ever heard of doublets these days. Labor costs too much. Might as well buy a synthetic the size you want and not worry about the balsam coming unstuck. No, mister, guess I can't help you. Now if it's real battle souvenirs or Maryland antiques you want, I got 'em."

I shook my head. "Thanks, but a one-bedroom apartment doesn't have the space those old farmhouses had. Got to watch every inch."

"Yeah," he said sourly, "an' they call that progress." His lips peeled back and he spat in a tarnished brass spittoon. A perfect ringer. "Drop by again," he called as I went down the cast-iron stairway. When I looked back he was whittling again, doing his imitation of Abner Peabody. An old con gone straight, and plenty the worse for it.

The Olds' upholstery was hot as an electric grill. I bought a newspaper folded it, and put it on the seat, hoping the fresh ink was set in the paper.

I crossed the Mall, drove west on Pennsylvania as far as Washington Circle, and took 23rd to Connecticut and out Columbia Road. The district had two neighborhood theaters, an appliance shop, a laundry, a confectioner's store, a saloon, two supermarkets, and an independent grocery that seemed to be feeling the pinch. A chain drugstore, a radio-TV shop that sold records, a fruit stand with an Italian restaurant above it, and a package store with a sign taped to the window: Call Us We Deliver.

When I found the store I was looking for it had two display windows divided by the entrance. In silver script across both windows sprawled the word Sabatini. The window glass was as clean and shiny as the Orrefors crystal displayed on the green velvet background. There were polished silver candelabra, christening cups, a rosewood chest with staggered trays showing table silver and beside it a modest card suggesting that young couples purchase same on "Easy Credit Terms."

Inside a hassock fan circulated air around your ankles. Great for the sandal and bare-leg crowd, but for me it was worse than useless. A thin scent of cologne hung in the air like light mist, diluting the expected odor of silver polish and moth crystals.

The store cases held wristwatches, strings of imitation pearls, costume jewelry, and a large selection of wedding and engagement rings. In the far Corner behind a small workbench sat a man wearing a jeweler's eyepiece. He had a high sloping forehead with long black hair slicked flat. At the temples it looked eaten away. He stood up, removed the eyepiece, and smiled. His teeth were wide and white. His skin was the color of weak tea and his nose curved down over a pencil mustache. In his white cord suit, blue shirt, and white silk tie he looked a little like Xavier Cugat. Walking behind the display cases, he reached a position across the display case from me and stopped. The floor fan flapped my cuffs against my ankles. A few doors away, on the sidewalk, three girls were playing hopscotch, but inside the store it was quiet.

The side of Sabatini's index finger smoothed moisture from his thin mustache and he said pleasantly, "May I show you something? An engagement ring perhaps? An anniversary gift?" His right hand slid aside the back of a display case and he began to lift out a tray of rings.

"That's rushing the season a little," I said. "I suppose you can cut and polish stones here?"

He nodded. "You have a particular stone in mind?"

Taking a pencil from my shirt pocket I tore a sheet from a note pad on the counter and began sketching an eight-sided stone, drawing concentric lines to suggest the step cut. When it was finished I pushed it across the glass toward him and he looked at it with interest.

"Could you make a stone like that?"

"Were you thinking of topaz perhaps? Amethyst?"

I shook my head. "The lady's eyes are green."

"Emerald? My God, it would cost a fortune."

I laughed embarrassedly. "Not real emerald, Mr. Sabatini—not all of it, anyway. Isn't there some way jewelers put a synthetic base on a real stone and make it look like the real thing?"

"Such a stone is called a doublet. But even a doublet of the size you have drawn would be worth twenty or thirty thousand dollars."

"Twenty thousand dollars." I murmured. "Well, I didn't have anything like that in mind. I was thinking of a flashy stone for, say, four or five hundred bucks."

He smiled condescendingly. "Even if it were possible to procure an emerald crown for the doublet, the crown alone would cost approximately fifteen thousand dollars. Time is required, also, to study the properties of the stone, the coloration, the cleavage lines and so forth. Diamonds are often X-rayed before being cut. Then a base—a synthetic or flawed emerald or a semiprecious stone of the exact color as the crown—must be found and cut. No, a doublet is not what you want, sir."

"I'll give it more thought," I told him, and took a business card from my billfold. "Give me a call if anything comes to mind."

He took the card, read it, and turned it idly in his fingers. "Even a topaz of that size and cut would cost more than the sum you mentioned. Perhaps something in the semi-precious field? Green tourmaline—what is called Brazilian emerald?"

"That's a thought," I said, "but it would have to look pretty convincing."

"It would," he said silkily. "I could promise you that."

Picking up my sketch, I fingered it, then dropped it under his gaze. "Prosperous-looking place you have here," I said. "Business good?"

"I can't complain." His eyes were having difficulty staying away from the sketch.

"Fine," I said. "Does my heart good to see a fellow doing well in a legitimate business. This day and age the temptation to cut a corner here and there must be almost irresistible."

"Meaning what, sir?"

"Only that a man with a clean conscience has nothing to worry about."

"Who are you?"

"My name's on my card."

He gazed at the sketch. His mouth opened and closed.

"Go on," I said.

"I have nothing to say."

"Funny, I thought you were going to say something more."

The smile was an effort. "What, for instance?"

"That the drawing looked familiar. It could easily be. After all, the size and cut are unique—in emeralds."

He looked up from the sketch. "I don't understand," he said in a strangled voice. "Some kind of joke?"

"Try harder," I said. "Throw a little schmaltz into it and be halfway convincing. You know the cut. You recognize the size and the stone—every jeweler does. Convince me you're the exception."

His nails clawed the glass counter. "Why did you come here? What is it you want to know?"

CHAPTER FIFTEEN

"I like it better the other way. You telling me. Look, I'm not even from the city pound, Mr. Sabatini. And you've told me what I wanted to know, don't think you haven't." I cupped the sketch in my hand and crumpled it. "The Madagascar Green," I said. "La Verde de Madagascar. Remember now?"

There was sweat on his forehead. "I'm clean," he said suddenly. "I swear it. You haven't anything on me. Nothing. I did my stretch, the hard way." His voice whined, "Let me alone. Can't you people get off my back?"

I lofted the crumpled sketch into a basket beyond the counter. "Why try to pretend you didn't know the Green?" I asked softly, turned and walked out of the store. When I looked back he had picked up my card and was staring at it.

I walked half a block to the saloon, drank a draft ale, and called Artie's office. He answered and said, "Excuse the chewing sound, Steve. Spiced beef and Swiss. On rye."

"You're supposed to be working on a case," I told him. "No time off for meals."

"Call this a meal?" he asked bitterly.

"Artie, that list of ex-con jewelers you gave me—any of them on the habit?"

"Maybe, maybe not. It'll take another check to find out. Want it?"

"Sure," I said, "so long as you're billing Mrs. Sewall."

"Billing you would be a waste of time."

I agreed and said, "So far, I've seen Louie Arnold and Pablo Sabatini. Louie's off the list entirely. I sketched the stone for Sabatini, and he recognized it but pretended he didn't. I left him my address."

"Why?"

"If he made the fake stone he might be worried enough to want to keep me from nosing around."

"Decoy, huh?"

"Call it that."

"What's Sabatini like?"

"I scratched him a little but nothing much happened. Just for fun I'll check Weiskold next."

"Don't get things too damn stirred up," Artie said irritably. "I'll let you know about the junkie angle in a couple of hours." He hung up.

I went back to the bar, hooked my heel on the brass rail, and sipped another draft ale. It was very cold indeed. By now Mrs. Bross would be back at her desk, so I could take my time.

From the bar I got into my car and drove back down Connecticut, around Sheridan Circle, and over into Georgetown. I parked beyond Wisconsin on the shady side of M Street and walked up and down the block looking for Max Weiskold's store.

When I found it, it was not a jewelry store at all. Instead, the window carried a double sign: Hobby Shop, and below it, the word Lapidary. The window display showed chunks of quartz and felspar, some polished cabochons in a cardboard tray, and cat's-eye and turquoise cabochons mounted in jewelry foundations as brooches, earrings, and novelty pins. There were also sections of petrified wood polished to show the yellow grain.

The inside of the store had bins and racks that held rough stones, labeled according to kind. Colored quartz mostly, carnelian, and pockets of colored stone still set in the natural crystal fragments.

The sidewalk awning had kept the shop reasonably cool. Behind the counter at a workbench sat a man. He was bent over a small power motor with a polishing head that was wet with oil and grinding compound. His right hand held a four-inch stick. At one end, imbedded in dopping wax, was a cabochon. His fingers rotated the cabochon against the polishing head. The only sound in the shop was the whirring of the electric motor.

I cleared my throat and the man looked up. He saw me, switched off the motor, and laid aside the dop stick. Then he got up slowly and came toward me. He was an old man with wild hair and deep-set eyes magnified by his thick glasses. Across one concave cheek was a smear of oil. His fingers looked gritty and his back hunched so far forward that he seemed to have no neck at all. His chest was flat and thin and his bony arms looked white and wasted.

He blinked at me like a bat suddenly coming into light, and said, "Something, gentleman?"

"Some Number one-twenty grit," I told him, "and a pinch of silicon compound."

"Certainly," he said, his head bobbing. "You have the hobby, gentleman?"

"When I get time," I told him, "which isn't often. Right now I'm polishing an agate cabochon for a ring."

"Beautiful," he said. "For a lady, is it?"

"For a lady," I agreed.

He turned away, dipped into his bins, and brought back two small bags. "One dollar-twenty," he said. "Something else, perhaps?"

"Well," I said, "the wife's got an old amethyst that's been lying around for years doing nobody any good. The only thing is it's kind of thin. I've been thinking maybe something could be made from it."

"Perhaps a brooch, gentleman?"

"That's what I've been thinking. The amethyst's big enough to make a crown only I don't think I'm good enough to cut and match a base for a doublet. I was wondering if you could maybe do it for me?"

Something flickered across his eyes. "A doublet, gentleman? Yes, I am able to do such work for you."

"I'd want a good job," I warned. "The stone's got a lot of sentimental value. My wife's grandmother brought it over from the Old Country—Germany."

"Chermany?" he said in a pleased way. "It was also my home. Until the Nazis." His mouth twisted. "Yes, I could make you a fine amethyst doublet, gentleman. My trade I learned in Amsterdam." His head turned and his eyes took in his shop. "I have cut diamonds and rubies even. But now…" His voice trailed away. "When could you bring it in?"

"Tomorrow?"

He nodded. "Tomorrow will be good."

I took out a business card and my pencil. On the back of my card I repeated the sketch I had done for Sabitini. When it was finished he bent forward, peered at it, and licked his lips. "It should be cut like so?" he asked in a hoarse whisper.

"Will it be hard to do?"

He seemed not to hear me.

"Can you make this kind of a doublet?" I asked.

His head raised slowly. "I do not know, gentleman," he husked. "So large a stone. Step cut, and—"

"The hell with technicalities," I said loudly. "If you can't, I'll take the work to someone else."

"No, no," he said suddenly. "I will do it. It is just…"

"How's that?"

"…just that the job is so large," he finished.

"Well," I said, "if you're sure you can handle it I'll bring around the stone tomorrow. How long will it take?"

His head turned and he peered at a wall calendar. Finally he said, "A week... better ten days. You have the time?"

I nodded, picked up my purchases, and walked out of the shop. Crossing the street, I went to a rubbish container and dropped the bags in it. Then I got into the Olds and drove back to my office.

I had baited two hooks. One of them might bring the fish I wanted.

A little before five Mrs. Bross told me a lady wanted to talk with me on the telephone and when I picked it up a voice said, "Mr. Bentley, I'm Janice Western. You remember me, don't you?"

"Sure do."

Her voice had a low, coaxing quality. "Have you got time to drop up for a drink? I've got something to tell you."

"Like what?"

"'Well, I'd prefer if you was here."

"It sounds all veiled and mysterious," I said. "I just might have time for one Tom Collins."

"Good. I'm in the Revere, off DuPont Circle. Five Four Two. About six?"

"Six'll be fine," I told her.

"See you," she said, and hung up.

Mrs. Bross left punctually. I lingered, puttering with papers on my desk, and when the hall door closed behind her I locked it and opened my safe. From one of the drawers I took out Guiseppe's 9 mm. pistol, shoved it into a quick-draw holster, and threaded it on my belt.

I dialed Artie's number but no one answered and when the answering service cut in I hung up. Prompt quitters, I thought, even though Artie hadn't called back with an answer to what I had asked him. Or perhaps there had not been a ready answer. Answers were at an all-time premium.

Leaving the office, I went down to the bar, swallowed a double Martini, thought of another, and decided it was a grand way to become a lush. A quick look at the other customers bore me out, and at a quarter to six I left.

I drove the Olds up toward DuPont Circle, turned off and parked in the driveway of the Revere Apartment-Hotel.

The lobby was cool and quiet, like the coffee lounge of one of those art theaters that show only foreign films—only twice as large—and decorated in the latest fashion. A desk clerk announced me upstairs and an elevator gave me a soundless ride to the fifth floor. The carpeting had more spring than a trampoline.

Janice Western answered the buzzer. She wore a crimson Chinese jacket, black toreador trousers, and jade earrings. A jade brooch was cut in the complicated form of a Chinese character. The heavy door closed on noiseless hinges and the apartment became as insulated from the outside world as a bank vault.

The wallpaper was largely saffron and rust. Against it in black silhouettes were bamboo fronds, broad-bladed spear heads, African shields, pangas, ceremonial fetishes, impalas, masks, and congo drums. In an excess of geographic license, boomerangs had been included.

"Back from the safari?" I asked.

She shook her head. "I been nowhere. Why?"

"It would make me nervous, all those eyes and deadly weapons."

She smiled and inserted a cigarette into a long silver holder. I lit it for her and she said, "I hold myself down to five cigs a day—on account of my voice."

"That would make me even more nervous."

We walked toward the furniture. One seat was saffron, the other rust. Solid colors, at least. From a tray she picked up a tall frosted glass and gave it to me. I sipped and said, "It helps kill the Sen-Sen."

She smiled again, in a vague sort of way, and made a gesture with her free hand. "This is my studio, too."

There was a small ebony-colored piano, on it a microphone that led toward a tape recorder set on a TV table.

"I can see you love your work," I ventured. "Were you planning to sing for me or shall we just turn on the recorder and have our music the easy way?

She shook her head and her face grew serious. "I got a confession to make. I should have talked before, but I couldn't. I just couldn't." She gazed at me but my face told her nothing.

"About what?"

Looking away, she said, "The Tracy Farnham killing."

"You did it?"

"Me? God, no." She laughed hollowly. "I didn't even know the man. I didn't have nothing against him."

I said, "If you know something about the murder I have a nodding acquaintance with a Lieutenant Kellaway of Homicide— if that'll help any."

"No...no. Not the cops. It'd kill me professionally if my name got into it."

"Professionally?" I asked. "Which profession, honey?"

She wanted to slap me but thought better of it. She grated, "My singing—as an entertainer. I can't get mixed in no murders."

"Then stay away from them," I suggested unhelpfully.

"Damn you, listen! I know who killed Tracy Farnham only I can't go to the police with it on account of my...my career," she finished.

"So you'll tell me instead, and let me carry the tidings. That about the size of it?"

"You'll do it, won't you? You'll tell them."

"It depends," I said, "on how I like the story. Who, for example, sapped Tracy Farnham and cut his throat with a switchblade knife last Monday afternoon—or evening?"

"Haven't you guessed?"

"No."

The back of her hand brushed moisture from her lip. She took a deep breath, leaned forward, and said, "Wayne Cutler. He killed Farnham, that's who did it."

"My, my," I said, and fished a cigarette from my coat, holding the coat front to hide the holstered automatic. I lit the cigarette and gazed at her. "I never would have thought it. I wrote him off long ago as just a harmless lush. A murderer, you say? That will bear looking into. By chance were you an eye witness?"

"No, of course I wasn't. I wasn't anywhere near the place. But Wayne was here that afternoon. I'd just told him it was all over between us. Finished, see? He took it hard. Then he tore out of here shouting he was going to kill Tracy Farnham."

"You were keeping Tracy or something?"

She glowered at me. "Tracy was hot for Sara—everybody knows that. Wayne must of gone to Tracy's apartment from here and killed Tracy." She fidgeted. "Sara was there that afternoon, you know."

"I know," I said. "Half the police force knows, too. But it didn't interest them much, Tracy having so many lady callers and such like."

She was just staring at me. Her face changed color a couple of times; her lips parted and her jaws moved but nothing came out. Her lips had gone dry and she licked them.

I put down my drink carefully, stood up and straightened my lapels. "Now I remember," I said thoughtfully. "I'm supposed not to like Wayne Cutler. Because I bought his lovely young wife a couple of drinks at the Bagatelle and he barged in and broke it up. Or I don't like rich young wastrels. That should make me a plausible source for the story. And there are other angles, too. For instance, Tracy was supposed to be coining gold with Iris, and Paul Sewall objected. Not a hell of a lot, but he liked a high gloss on his property so long as it belonged to him. Add Sara, and that makes Tracy quite a lad with the ladies. You didn't know him so that's one he missed. Too bad, because he could have done a duet with you—the easiest flop in town."

She slammed the drink at me, but I was expecting it and ducked. It broke behind me and dripped down against the nightmare wall paper. I took a step toward her and said, "Dearie, you want to think twice before you do a thing like that again. I haven't finished talking yet, and you'll be even madder. So, as I was saying, the only guy really hot after Sara is Paul Sewall— hot enough to divorce Iris on the off chance of getting Sara to consent. Only Sara's back with Wayne again. That's probably subject to change, but at the moment they're living together. Let's say Paul's getting a little eager—too eager to be discreet. He wants to hang Farnham's murder on Wayne Cutler as the way to a quick disposal. Then marry the widow. The story's old, a frayed cliché. Then on top of that, Paul might have one other reason for interesting Vance Bodine in hanging the Farnham murder on Wayne Cutler: Sewall knows, or suspects, who the real murderer is and realizes that Bodine has to protect him. A double-barrel promotion. Slick."

I took a deep breath and held up my hand but it wasn't necessary; there was no fight left in her. Her skin was sallow, her eyes sunken.

"You're picked to start the ball rolling—with me, for reasons I mentioned previously—and you can't refuse. Why not? Because you got orders from the guy who rigged this witch doctor's hut for you—Vance Bodine. So call Vance and say it didn't work. The scheme was perfect except the payoff. This sort of leaves it with you having to call in the cops yourself and make a sworn statement. But remember the perjury laws, dearie, and don't make it too strong. Learn from the shysters and always leave a loophole. You can do it. Blink the phony eyelashes and mutter indistinctly and you've got it made. If I've been brutally frank it's because I can't stomach the frame you we're trying to pull. I like it even less knowing Bodine's behind it."

I turned and walked away from her. As far as the vault-like door. With my hand on the knob I glanced back and said, "Maybe I should have played it smooth, let you think I swallowed the story and was making a bee-line for the nearest cop to stutter it all out the way you told it. Now I'm really dangerous to Sewall and Bodine. They're protecting a murderer, so now they have to stop me. I wonder if they will."

She screamed at me; not words, just a hoarse, raging screech. I opened the door and went out into the corridor. The elevator door opened and I stepped in. All the way to the lobby her scream echoed in my ears.

CHAPTER SIXTEEN

Back in my apartment, I mixed a long Scotch to steady myself, shed my wringing clothes, and stood in my shorts until the cool air helped me stop sweating. I took the Czech automatic out of its holster, sprang the clip, and checked the cartridges. All there. Soft-nose bullets with copper jackets that could tear the leg off a horse. Replacing the clip, I slid the pistol back into the spring holster. I wondered who would come for me tonight—Sabatini, Cokey Joe, or Cadena himself.

When my hand was steady I dialed Oscar Calvo's Fiesta Shop number. The phone rang a long time but no one answered. I hung up, then dialed Oscar's apartment over the shop. No answer there, either. Out somewhere. Out on the town. Cultivating contacts probably. Young, impressionable contacts. Like Silvio Contreras, for instance. Friends bound by the ties of language and country.

Dialing Police Headquarters, I asked for Homicide and learned that Detective Lieutenant Kellaway had checked out home for the night. Would someone else do? No, no one else would do. It was Kellaway's show.

By degrees I got dressed again, still feeling shaky inside, but I had done my night's drinking. Enough for a lifetime, maybe. I was tying a bow tie when the telephone rang. It was Artie and his voice was tired and a little thick. He said, "Buddy, you wanted the name of any jeweler on that list who was a junkie, didn't you?"

"Who was it?"

"Two. Weiskold got the habit in concentration camp but shook it before he got over to this country. Sabatini took the snow cure along with his first sentence. The police know he puffs a muggle or so now and then but they leave him alone so they can keep track of the pusher. According to the Narcotics boys, Sabatini's clean."

"It couldn't have been just one," I said disgustedly. "It had to be two."

"Maybe cutting stones makes a guy nervous," he suggested. "You doing any good for me?"

"No," I said. "It's your basket of worms from now on."

"Say," he said, his voice rising a little, "something bothering you?"

"Murder," I said. "A case of murder. Or two."

"You a little drunkie, maybe?"

"It's that time of day," I said, and hung up.

Outside the sky was nearly dark. The street lights went on and car headlights looked like fireflies gliding silently down the hill. From the apartment below came the loud blasting of a TV Western.

I finished tying my bow tie, threaded the holster back on my belt. It felt solid and comforting. Packing my pipe, I tried to hold a match and replaced the pipe in its rack. Great shape, I told myself. A few harsh words with a blonde bosco and you're all fretted up. Or possibly there was more to it than that. Just possibly.

The book from Brentano's was lying on the shelf jeering at me. I had an impulse to open the window and throw it as far as I could. Mr. Know Everything Bentley and all his technical knowledge.

Just then the door buzzer sounded. I pulled out the automatic and snicked a shell into the chamber. Walking quietly, I crossed the living room, going toward the door. Instead of standing in front of the door panel and turning the knob I kept behind the wall, except for my right hand. The hand that held the pistol.

I sucked in a deep breath just as firing broke out from the TV set downstairs. With my thumb and middle finger I grasped the knob and the pistol rattled against it. I began to turn the knob.

From the other side of the door came three loud reports and splintered holes ripped the door panel. In the center, where my body should have been. I stared at them, numb for a moment, then breath groaned out of my lungs and I hit the floor on my knees. Heavily. As though my dead body were falling.

Outside I heard a grunt, then feet began pounding away from me down the corridor. The TV firing had stopped and I could hear the running feet clearly. They ran past the elevator, turned in at the fire escape door. Then there was silence.

Leaning against the wall, I pushed myself to my feet. Snapping on the safety, I jammed the pistol back into my holster and opened the door. The bottom edge ground fallen splinters into the rug with a grating, snapping sound. On the outside of the panel the three holes were round and neat. They were not six inches apart and if I had been standing on the other side of the door the bullets would have gone through me.

There was sweat on my face, icy sweat, and I needed a drink worse than ever, but the time for that was long past. Stepping into the corridor, I closed the door and the spring lock snapped shut. As I jogged away no doors opened, no faces stared at me. The TV shooting had covered the sounds of the gunman's shots. I wondered if he had planned it that way.

The elevator was going down. It stopped for me and let me off in the lobby. I waited a moment, turned and walked to the fire escape door, opened it, and crossed the base of the fire stairs. The outside door was just closing. I felt weightless, moving through a dream. If I wanted to overtake the killer I could. Only I had another idea.

I pushed the door open a crack and saw a man running across the service area. He wore a dark suit and a felt hat. The front of his coat flapped behind him as he ran. The lights were too dim to see his face.

Pushing through the door, I slid outside, keeping next to the building until I could reach my Olds. The running man had crossed the hardtop and reached the sidewalk. He slowed to a jog, then walked with long quick strides until he was out of sight. Without turning on the headlights I started the engine and nosed the car slowly ahead until the front wheels were even with the sidewalk.

He was a block away, getting into a parked car on the other side of the street. I heard the engine start and the tires snarled as the car swung away from the curb. The car was a brown Plymouth coupé, three or four years old. It passed me like a streak, but not before I glimpsed the driver's face, a thin face with a hooked nose. The hat would be dove-gray. He braked for the intersection stop sign and I eased the Olds into the street, headlights on.

He turned down Massachusetts and I followed. He was holding the speed limit and traffic was scattered. At Wisconsin he made the light but it caught me. When I spotted his tail lights again he was passing Holy Rood Cemetery. At 35th Street he swerved over toward the river and stayed on it all the way to M Street. Two blocks on M and the brown Plymouth pulled over to the curb and the tail lights blinked out. He was crossing the street when I passed behind him. His gait was quick and nervous. A wiry man, tense and excited. I saw where he was headed, coasted another block, and braked the Olds against the curb a few doors from Wisconsin.

Crossing the street, I walked back, but he had vanished. It didn't make any difference because I knew now where he had gone. I ducked up a rat alley that led to the trash areas behind the stores, turned and walked behind the buildings until I reached the back of Max Weiskold's store.

The window shades were drawn but a crack of light showed through at one side of the window. Inside the back room there were three men. I heard Tip Cadena laugh harshly. Then he said, "Just like that, Giuseppe. You gave it to him through the door?"

"Yeah, Tip. Through the door." He laughed. It was a thin, gloating laugh. "In the belly."

"Good work," Cadena said. "Better tell Vance, Giuseppe."

"Right now?"

"Hell, yes. I can handle this old fool."

Cokey Joe snickered. "Looks like he wants a jolt, don't he? You gonna let him have his jolt, Tip?"

"Maybe," Cadena said. "He's got work to do first. A little work, eh, Max? Then your jolt."

Max Weiskold was sitting in a chair peering up at Cadena. His face was white and covered with sweat.

Cadena said, "You stalled long enough, Maxy. Days it's been and always some lousy excuse. I even get the idea you ain't interested in cuttin' the Green for me. But that's over now, ain't it? All over."

Max wiped his mouth on his forearm. When he spoke his voice was only a hoarse squeak. "Time it takes. Time. A little more time, gentleman. Then a perfect job I can do. Tomorrow..." His voice trailed away.

"You said that. You said it all before. So I'm sick hearing how much time it takes. Maxy, you ain't had a jolt all day. Well, you ain't gonna get one until that stone's cut. Understand? No more stalling."

From his coat pocket Cadena took out a small folded square of tissue paper that bulged slightly. "This's it, Maxy. It'll feel real good—better'n it ever felt before. So get out the Green and start working."

Max Weiskold's mouth was working. Like a man long deprived of water. Through the thick lenses his eyes looked large and bright, like a bird's.

Cokey Joe giggled again. "Tip, we oughta slap him around a while. What the hell you want to waste time on him for?"

"Easy," Cadena said, turning to him. "Easy now." He looked down at Max Weiskold. "You wouldn't want anything like that, would you, Maxy? Giuseppe here'd like to snap a few of your fingers, but I say no. So you'll do the job. You'll do it right and then you'll get that little jolt."

He leaned forward and stuck the tissue paper deck under Weiskold's nose. Tears were streaming down the old man's face. His fingers curled like claws. His scrawny neck craned forward and his nostrils twitched.

Cokey Joe muttered, "Hell, Tip, the time you waste!"

Cadena whirled around. "On your way, junkie. Out to Vance's like I said."

"Yeah. Okay. I'm goin'." He turned and walked to the doorway that opened into the front of the shop. The door opened and closed and Cadena turned to Weiskold.

"There's just us now, old man," he purred. "Just the two of us here. You wantin' the jolt worse than a trip to kosher heaven, and me with the jolt ready and waitin'."

He laid the deck down on a workbench near a grinding wheel. "Time, you said. Well, Maxy, I got plenty of time. That's all it takes. Look at it, old man. Stare at it and lick your lips. Think how good it'll feel when it hits. Warm and mellow."

Weiskold was trying to blot the tears from his cheeks. "Now," he said. "Give it to me now!"

"Now?" Cadena taunted. "You'd be outa this world for hours. The Green's gotta be cut, Maxy. Tonight. Now. You don't need the deck so bad. You get the wheel turning and we'll see."

Weiskold's fingers were at his throat.

Cadena smiled at him. "Get it out, Maxy. Turn the wheel and start work. I ain't seen the Green in a long time. Where you been keepin' it hid?"

Weiskold's hand snatched at the deck but Cadena's palm struck the side of his face, knocking him out of the chair. Cadena towered over him, rage in his face. "The Green," he shouted. "Get it!"

Max Weiskold got to his knees and stared up at Cadena. His lips moved but no words came out. Cadena slapped him again. The crack was like wet leather against steel. The old man's glasses were on the floor. He groped for them but Cadena toed them away. On his hands and knees Weiskold searched for them. He was crying.

Cadena kicked the glasses under the workbench.

I left the window and ran to the rear door. Through the door window I saw a dark hallway the length of the building. The door was unlocked. I turned the knob and stepped in, closing the door softly. The door to the back room was a few feet farther inside. A solid door. Pulling the automatic, I pushed off the safety and tiptoed to the door. Through the panel came the sound of blows, and of a defenseless old man pleading for mercy.

I put my left hand on the knob, opened the door, and said, "Cadena."

He whirled, saw the gun, and dove for his. He was halfway to his knees, trying to get it out, when I shot him. If he had been standing the slug would have caught him in the belly. It spun him around and knocked him backward. His pistol clattered against the floor. He lay on his back, the fingers of his left hand clawing at the wound. Blood crept between his fingers, staining the ice-cream suit.

"Friend," I said, "you're bleeding."

Max Weiskold had stopped searching for his glasses. He was on his hands and knees staring up at me. His lips were bloodless.

I went over to the workbench, bent down and picked up his glasses. I pressed them into his hand.

Cadena had rolled over on one side, moaning hoarsely. Out of the corner of my eye I could see Weiskold. He was standing up now, the tissue paper in the palm of one hand, unfolded. There was a silver spoon in the other. He was measuring white crystals into the spoon. Some of them spilled over the edge of the spoon and onto the floor. I bent over Cadena, grabbed his collar, and hoisted him until he was sitting up, rocking with pain.

"Grit your teeth, friend," I said. "The worst hasn't even begun."

"A doc," he gasped. "Get a doc. I'm bleedin' to death."

"Pathetic," I said. "Tracy Farnham bled to death while you watched. Fine. You're bleeding to death, too. What am I supposed to do? Bind the wound and pat your hot forehead with cool cloths?"

Weiskold had a bottle of something. His fingers were shaking, but he managed to get a few drops into the spoon. On the workbench lay a hypodermic syringe. I turned away.

Cadena was inching toward his gun.

I bent over and picked it up. "Too late," I said. "Much too late. You're dying, friend. Dying the way Tracy Farnham died."

"You got to get me a doc," he begged.

I glanced at Cadena's gun. A Spanish Astra. The receiver was engraved and chased with silver in scrollwork tracery. I stared at Cadena's eyes and said, "You should have got it in the belly, friend. The way you planned it for me. There's still a chance for you, just a chance, but time's short. You killed Tracy Farnham. Why?"

He groaned, shook his head, and said, "He found out about Oscar."

"Details," I said thickly. "He found out what? That Oscar took the emerald from Silvio?"

"Yeah. No. Farnham didn't know where it came from. He just knew Oscar had it."

"How?"

He wiped his lips with the back of the only hand he could use. "A doc," he moaned. "I'm dyin'."

"How did Farnham find out Oscar had the emerald?"

Cadena leaned back against a leg of the workbench. "He owed Farnham money—from the business. Farnham was squeezin' him to pay, an' he showed the stone. Said Farnham'd get his dough from it. But Farnham got greedy, wanted a bigger cut. Oscar checked with me, I told Vance, the answer was no."

I glanced over at Weiskold. Around his left arm he had bound a rag tourniquet. His right hand held the hypodermic syringe. The needle was imbedded in a distended vein and his eyes were closed.

I felt a little sick. Turning to Cadena, I said, "Silvio brought in dope each time he came. He passed it to Oscar. Who got it next, Cadena. You?"

His head nodded.

I said, "Whose idea was it to steal the Madagascar Green?"

"Vance's. But Oscar was willing."

"What about the old guy here? Who found him?"

"The guinea," he gasped.

"Oscar killed Silvio?"

"He says no. Says the guy was dead when he found him." He was rocking from side to side. The blood was dripping from his cuff to the floor.

Against the wall there was an iron cot. I saw Weiskold stumble toward it. He pulled back a quilt and lay down. One hand pulled off his glasses and laid them on the floor by his hand. His eyes closed.

Cadena's breath rattled like gravel against board. His eyes pleaded with me.

I said, "Why don't I just call Vance and let him send a doc, Tip? He's your buddy, isn't he?"

"No ... no. He'd let me die. Bentley, he'd kill me now."

I nodded slowly. "Remember that, friend," I told him. "Remember that when you're on the stand."

"The doc now. I told you everything."

I opened the door into the shop, saw the front shades were closed, and turned on the ceiling light. In the phone book I found Kellaway's number. After three rings he answered.

"Lieutenant Kellaway," he said, with a trace of irritation.

"Steve Bentley," I said. "Put on your shoes and get a meat wagon over here. Cadena's on the floor with a bad shoulder from a soft-nosed slug. Mine. Only don't tell it that way."

"How should I tell it?" he snapped.

"Giuseppe. He's on the road to Vance Bodine's. Brown Plymouth coupé. Unless he's ditched his gun it'll be short three cartridges. Pick him up for speeding and find out. As for Cadena, he's been singing like Lanza. He's lost some blood and he thinks he's dying. Bring along a couple of witnesses and have him tell you how he killed Tracy Farnham. There may be some chatter about an emerald, but pay no attention to it. Cadena can tell you considerable about the local drug picture, too. That diplomatic courier brought the stuff in. No customs to go through. Easy. And while you're at it, you might sound out Cadena on the rest of the rackets he ran for Bodine. It could be an interesting night for you, Lieutenant."

There was a pause. After a while, he said, "This straight stuff?"

"Hell," I said, "Cadena's here. Come over and ask him."

"Address?"

I gave it to him and said, "The owner's a little old refugee named Max Weiskold, one of your stoolies. He got the habit in Germany under the Nazis so I wouldn't go too hard on him, Lieutenant. The boys gave him quite a beating; he won't be talking until morning. When he does, he'll be too confused to remember how Giuseppe and Cadena broke in to rob his shop and shot it out over the loot. You might want to remind him."

"Asking quite a lot, aren't you?"

"Not so much," I said. "Compared to what you're getting out of it, nothing at all."

"All right. I'm on my way. You'll be there?"

"Giuseppe shot Cadena, Lieutenant. Why would I be here at all?"

"Figures," he barked, and slammed down the phone.

I put down the receiver and walked back into the other room. Cadena lay on his side, his eyes closed. I went over to him, knelt down, and felt for his heart. The beat was there. Nothing spectacular, but you could feel it.

I got his Astra out of my pocket, wiped it clean, and laid it on the workbench behind the electric motor. Then I turned and went over to the cot. Shaking Weiskold's shoulder, I said, "The emerald, Max. I came for it. Where is it?"

He thrashed a little and I shook him some more. He was a long way away, halfway to Nirvana, but maybe I could delay him just long enough.

"Max!" I shouted in his ear. "The emerald. Where did you hide it?"

Something like a smile came over his lips. His eyelids flickered but they stayed shut. His mouth opened and I leaned close to catch the words.

"So beautiful," he murmured, and there was a world of contentment in the whisper. "So beautiful, gentleman. Too beautiful to destroy."

"Yes," I said. "I know. But where is it now?"

I had to shake him again. When he spoke, the whisper was even softer than before, and the words were blurred.

"With the quartz," he said thickly. "At the bottom—the Serpentine quartz."

I got up and walked to the front of the shop. Reading the bin labels, I found one and pulled it out. The crystal prisms glinted in the light as I took out the chunks of rock quartz. Nodes of green stone were inside each chunk of quartz, rough and imperfect. Not even semi-precious stones. Cheap. Something for hobbyists to play with. A sharp crystal cut my left hand. I licked the gash and kept on lifting out stones.

At the bottom of the bin I found what I wanted. Only the green egg was perfectly shaped. It was set into the quartz, exposed as though the chunk had fractured that way. I stood up, held it toward the light, and saw a thin layer of white sandwiched under the bottom. It was set in a plaster of Paris matrix, the cut face down. The exposed side had been coated with something to dull it, conceal its perfection. With a coin I pried it gently out of its bed and held it toward the light. White fragments still clung to the stepped facets but they would soak off easily. The Madagascar Green.

I gazed at it, half-hypnotized, seeing the light sparkle from its facets, the infinite lustrous depth, like a bottomless green sea. To break away I had to shake my head.

CHAPTER SEVENTEEN

Slipping the emerald into my trouser pocket, I turned off the overhead light, dialed Iris Sewall's number, and told her to meet me at Uncle Oscar's store.

Waiting a moment, I dialed Oscar Calvo's apartment. He must have been waiting beside the phone because he answered before the first ring ended, and I said, "Oscar, this is Steve Bentley. Just letting you know Iris and I will be up to see you shortly. I'm bringing her along as a representative of your family to hear what you have to say about Silvio and the Madagascar Green. Cadena's in police custody, spilling like a waterfall and the emerald's where it ought to be. This gives you a few minutes to figure out where you stand. A fertile mind like yours ought to reach one or two conclusions by the time we get there."

I heard a gasp, and then the connection broke off. I replaced the receiver and walked through the half-darkness into the back room. Cadena's eyes were still closed. When I put my hand in front of his face his breath was barely strong enough to move smoke.

At the door I looked back at the old man sleeping on the iron cot and the unconscious man on the floor, the workbench with the electric motor and its bronze cutting discs, the Astra near it, and the blood on the floor.

Closing the door, I wiped my prints from the knob and went out into the trash alley. As I walked away from Wisconsin I heard the rising wail of a siren. It grew in pitch and volume until the car growled to a stop in front of Max Weiskold's store.

As I emerged from the alley I saw a policeman put his shoulder to the front door and burst through. Flashlights went on, darting around the store, then headed toward the back of the shop.

I crossed M Street, walked back toward Wisconsin, and got into my Olds. Just then an ambulance from Georgetown Hospital careened around the corner and screeched to a lurching stop behind the prowl car.

I started the Olds and turned up Wisconsin to Q Street. There was hardly any traffic. Along the sidewalk a few people were running after the ambulance. Busy-bodies hoping to see blood. There was enough for everybody tonight.

I fished a cigarette out of a crumbled pack and lighted it with a shaking hand. Q Street was quiet. A thin breeze rustled the elm leaves overhead. It was the only sign of life.

Parking across from The Fiesta Shop I turned off the headlights and waited. Oscar had forgotten to turn on the display lights and the front windows were dark. Above the shop a dim light showed in the front window of the walk-up. I wondered how he was taking it all.

I saw her Lancia then, pulling toward me like a blood-red bullet. She parked in front of the shop, turned off the headlights, and looked around. I got out of the Olds and crossed the street to her. She was wearing the brocade lounging pajamas I had seen once before. Around her hair she had tied a gauzy silver handkerchief.

"Well," she said, "why all the mystery?"

I put my hands on the door and leaned on them to steady myself. "I didn't really intend to be mysterious; I was just pressed for time."

From my pocket I took out the Madagascar Green. "Here it is, baby," I said wearily. "Two corpses later."

Her hand reached up and took it from me. She cradled it gently in her palm. "Where did you get it?"

"That'll keep. Right now let's pay a call on the man who took it."

Her other hand covered the emerald, caressed it softly, and fear came into her eyes. Her head tilted upward until she was staring at the lighted window above. She said, "You don't mean ... Steve, it wasn't my ..."

"Uncle Oscar," I finished. "We'll assume he took it from Silvio—his young friend Silvio, the junkie. Uncle Oscar, in and out of the Embassy at will, meeting everyone, aware of everything that was going on. Silvio would have known about the emerald from the pouch manifest—and he had the combination to your father's safe. I think he stole it for Oscar because he had to— because your uncle knew him for what he was, a drug addict, and could have exposed him. Oscar knew because Silvio worked for him. Not at The Fiesta Shop, Iris. Not selling herbs and bad turquoise, but they were in business together just the same. The drug business. One of Vance Bodine's sidelines, a line of business he delegated to Tip Cadena."

Her lips moved but no sound came out.

"Silvio was an addict," I repeated. "He brought drugs here from South America, slid them through Customs because of his Diplomatic Immunity—the kind all couriers have. Once here, Silvio turned over the hop to Oscar, who passed it to Tip Cadena for cutting and pushing."

"Steve—you can't know what you're saying!"

I shrugged. "Baby, I'm not just making it up. I'm telling you how it was. Oscar knew a jeweler here in town—a pitiful old man who depended on Oscar for his drugs. Oscar didn't have any way to peddle the emerald after it was cut, so Cadena probably handled that part—Cadena would know how those things were done. So that made five men connected to the theft: Silvio, Vance Bodine, Oscar, Cadena, and the jeweler who was the last to know. But a sixth found out—Tracy Farnham."

"Tracy knew?"

I nodded. "And knowing got him killed—by Cadena. I don't know how much a little shop like this one makes—or loses—but according to Cadena your Uncle Oscar owed Tracy some money. Too bad Tracy didn't have a more generous nature, because he kept pressing Oscar for the money and Oscar couldn't pay; he made Oscar so desperate that when Oscar got his hands on the Madagascar Green he showed it to Tracy by way of proving he could pay Tracy whatever it was he owed him. That made Tracy greedy for big money. But Oscar told Cadena and Cadena got orders from Bodine to cut Tracy's throat to keep him quiet."

She was biting the back of one hand to keep from screaming.

"The knife the police found up in Montrose Park, well, a stoolie says it was Cadena's, but the police couldn't get him to say so in a court where Cadena's bolos could see his face and shoot him down the next time they saw him. Maybe Cadena heard the knife had been picked up, maybe his information wasn't that good. Anyway, he must have been getting nervous because Bodine tried to frame someone else for Tracy's murder. It was a bad try because the people who engineered it assumed I had reason to hate the man who was supposed to be framed—Wayne Cutler."

I took a deep breath and glanced up at the light. Oscar was reading maybe, or going over the day's books. At least he was there.

I said, "A child could have seen through the fable Miss Janice Western tried to persuade me to repeat to the police, and I let her know it. Among other things, I let her know I was aware Cadena had killed Farnham and I did it for a reason—to make Cadena finally come after me."

"You did that?"

"He would have come sooner or later anyway. I think Bodine was suspicious of me pretty early in the game, and one night at the Bagatelle Cadena had reason to confirm those suspicions. Anyway, Cadena sent one of his hophead monkeys to do the job, but I was sort of expecting it and so I didn't get hurt. The gunman thought I was dead though, and sailed off to report to Cadena. I followed him to a little shop down on M Street. Cadena was there trying to bully the jeweler into cutting the Madagascar Green. The old guy was used to beatings, and he was enough of an Old World artisan to flinch from destroying a jewel as perfect as the stone in your hand. He'd stalled Cadena for days, fortunately, and Cadena was taking it out on him when I broke it up."

I gestured with my head. "Cadena's back there now with a hole in his shoulder the size of a baseball and minus a couple of quarts of blood. He'll live long enough to burn for Tracy's murder, and in his weakened condition he ought to be willing to murmur considerable of interest concerning Vance Bodine's assorted interests, including the Madagascar Green. Enough to finish Bodine."

I wiped my sleeve across my forehead. "Your family has another score against Bodine. He set about ruining Wayne Cutler, probably with crooked dice, and nearly succeeded. He wanted Wayne's lands, and it would be a favor to Paul Sewall. Because Sewall wants your sister, and with Cutler on the trash pile it looked a lot easier. I think Sewall must have been the one who got Bodine to try to frame Wayne through Janice and me, and Bodine would have gone along with it because Wayne had got out from under him financially and he needed a fall guy to save his lieutenant, Cadena. In any case, that's the kind of a husband you have." I didn't add that I'd once suspected Wayne of being involved in the theft.

Her hand fumbled with a small pocket in the brocade and she slipped the Madagascar Green into it. Under the streetlight her face was the color of parchment.

I said, "All of which brings us back to your uncle here. He had Silvio in his power through drugs, and through the threat of exposure to your father. After Silvio stole the emerald Oscar arranged to get it from him at the Hotel Flora. I think he planned to murder Silvio there because he could have got the stone from him at the Mayflower where he was staying, or on the street, for that matter, but the background had to look right. I think Oscar went to the Flora and got the emerald from Silvio as planned. I think he offered to mix a jolt for Silvio in what was to appear as a burst of friendly generosity, and mixed a killing dose. I think he punctured Silvio's arm with the needle and helped him lie down on the bed—to die. None of this can be proved unless Oscar wants to give us the details. While Silvio was dying Oscar ripped the room apart to make it look as though some junkie was frantically trying to find Silvio's cache of morphine. Or, less likely, Silvio was holding out on Oscar for more drugs or money, and Oscar had to search the room until he found the Madagascar Green. But find it he did and he left the place knowing the stage setting was right for what Silvio's death was supposed to look like—suicide or death by misadventure on the part of a man who had wrecked his life with dope and regretted it."

Her voice was parched. "Why are you telling me all this?"

"You're the big sister, Iris. I think if you know the facts you'll know what to do. You won't want to tell your father everything, of course, but you'll have to tell him something when you return the emerald and explain about the doublet he thinks is the real thing. And you'll have to ease the blow of Oscar. So now that you know what you do I thought we might go up and see what Oscar has to say."

I opened the car door and helped her onto the sidewalk. She stood for a moment, staring at me, and then her eyes traveled upward until she could see the lighted window. "Can't I see him alone?" she asked.

I shook my head. "Bodine pulled the strings, but Oscar was ready and willing to ruin his own brother," I told her. "Think he'd let you stand between him and freedom?"

"Do you have to—I mean, since Cadena's already caught can't you just—?"

"Let him go?" I finished. "Ignore the whole thing?" I shook my head. "I hoped you wouldn't ask that, Iris. I'd have a lot more respect for you if you'd been able to realize the law's the same for him as it is for Cadena. I don't think even your father would ask what you've just asked me to do."

Her shoulders slumped then, and she turned away and crossed the sidewalk. I followed until we were in front of the entrance door that opened on the stairway to the second floor. Oscar Calvo, the smudged card over the doorbell said. Her hand reached for it, but I pushed it aside. "He's expecting us."

There was light showing through the curtained window at the head of the stairs. When we got there, Iris knocked on the window glass and we waited for a moment, then she knocked again. There was no sound of movement within. I reached beyond her and turned the door knob. It opened inward, but then she hesitated and said, "Do you think it's right just to walk in?"

"He can always file a complaint."

The flat was unimpressive. Overstuffed furniture, shabby and stained from wear, the kind that is bought at eviction sales. Maple tables and chairs, an old radio, a small TV set, magazines in Spanish. The single lighted lamp had a paper shade with a design of anchors and sailing ships. Gay, hopeful illusion. But Oscar Calvo's ship had never come in.

I said, "Every time your uncle came back here after visiting the Embassy he must have made unkind comparisons. The only times I ever saw him he impressed me as a man eaten alive by something. I'd guess it was envy."

"Please don't say anything more," she asked in a voice that was guarded and uneven.

I looked around the room and took the automatic out of the holster. Slipping off the safety catch, I said, "He might just be back in the kitchen."

The breath caught in her throat and I saw her staring at the gun. "You wouldn't," she said. "Steve ..."

"He has to pay sometime. If he rushes me it'll be quick, and for your sake, better. I happen to admire your father, Iris. The police will co-operate as much as they can in keeping the Madagascar Green out of the papers; it's Oscar you want to worry about."

I turned and walked toward the dark hallway. On the left was a dark bedroom. No one on the bed asleep. The next room was a bathroom. I reached inside and turned on the ceiling light. Nothing there but porcelain and tile. I moved from it and the light shined into the kitchen, illuminating it dimly.

There was enough light to cast shadows. From the table, from the chair strangely overturned on the floor. From the shoes dangling two feet above the floor. I felt my heart stop, then start again. Shoving the gun back into the holster, I walked to the kitchen doorway and looked up.

Across one side of the ceiling led a three-inch water pipe. A rope had been thrown over it and knotted tight. The end hung tautly downward, ending at the neck of the man suspended by it. The neck was oddly twisted, the head lay at an oblique angle to the shoulders. The eyes were popped and staring, the teeth clamped on the protruding, bitten tongue. The arms hung like the slack limbs of a lifeless marionette.

I stepped backward, fighting to turn from the sight, and my fingers found the bathroom switch and the light went out. I leaned weakly against the wall, and after a while I made my way back into the room where Iris was waiting.

She looked at me curiously and said, "You look as if you'd just seen a ghost."

"I have."

Lines of white appeared on her cheekbones. She tried to rush past me, but I held her until she went limp in my arms. Finally she turned from me wordlessly and went out of the door. I closed it, hearing her stumbling steps, and caught up with her on the sidewalk.

"Can you make it to the Embassy?"

She nodded, opened the door of her Lancia and got in.

I stood watching it pull away from the curb and then I crossed the street and got into the Olds.

The cigarette tasted like old burlap but it was part of life, something real. The dim light on the second floor was a wake lamp for the dead. I stared at it for a long time and then forced myself to turn the key and start the engine. The noise broke the spell and I drove away.

I was waiting for her when the Lancia purred into the sunken garage. From her pocket she took the door key and pressed it into my hand, as though she were expecting me. I opened the door and followed her inside. A single lamp burned with a muted glow. Against the background the Siamese cat was invisible. All but the pale blue eyes.

Her fingers worried the silver gauze from her hair and then her shoulders slumped tiredly. She said, "I'm glad you came. I was wondering how I'd face it alone."

"Drink?"

"Please."

There was enough ice left in the bucket for two drinks, mostly Scotch. I carried one over to her on the beige sofa. Sitting beside her, I took a long deep breath and said, "It isn't every week I run into two of the most beautiful women in the world, Iris, stumble over two dead bodies—or shoot a man, for that matter."

Her voice was a little stronger. Part of the self-composure had returned. She said, "What are you trying to say, Steve?"

I touched my glass to hers. "Here's to the end of the line."

Her fingers touched the side of my face. She said, "You're getting off?"

"It seems like the thing to do."

"I'm sorry. I've always thought we could have a wonderful time together."

"That's the trouble. We could. But I could get to liking it too much. Me and my vulnerable ticker."

"What about mine?"

"I'm not sure," I said, "but I sort of figured you kept it in an armored car."

Her lips brushed mine. "Wrong, darling. So very, very wrong. Wouldn't you reconsider?"

"I'll be reconsidering for a long time," I told her. "Every time I drop into Hogan's and you're not there. Every time someone orders Pimm's Number One Cup."

"Little things," she mused. "But I'll remember too. Believe me, I'll remember."

"Thanks," I said. "I'll feel as though the circus left town."

"That's a nice way of saying it, Steve." Her lips kissed the side of my mouth. I kissed her back and then I lighted a cigarette and said, "Men aren't born equal, no matter what the Constitution says. Not equal in brains, talents, or abilities. If your uncle had been born with more of any one quality he wouldn't have had to become what he was."

"You don't have to apologize for him, not to me. I've acknowledged what he was. Nothing can change it."

I let smoke drift toward the cat's distant milky eyes. "He suffered from comparison," I remarked. "Compared to your father he was nothing. Nothing at all. That kind of realization has ruined much stronger men. Let's say it drove him into the dope racket, into the hands of Vance Bodine through Tip Cadena. Vance would have picked out Oscar's vulnerabilities just as a matter of routine. I see Vance Bodine playing on your uncle's gnawing envy of your father, persuading him to arrange the theft through Silvio. Bodine has the brains and the brilliance to do it—of all of them he's the only one who did. All the tools were there—even Cadena was his creature. Bodine was the spider at the center of the web, your uncle was only a trapped, miserable fly."

"Why are you saying all this? To cushion the fact that my uncle—my own blood—was a criminal?"

"Partly," I said. "And to make you realize the secondary part he played."

In the quietness of the room I could hear her breathing. It grew even, regular, almost relaxed. I got up from the sofa and finished my drink. She drew up her legs and lay back against a cushion.

"I'll call Artie in the morning," I said. "Give him the details."

Her eyes were half-closed, dreamy. The contours of her face had filled again, and her lips were parted in a detached expression that was close to indifference. I wondered if she had heard me at all, if any of what I had been saying had reached through and touched her, penetrated the lacquered armor. When I put down my glass the slight noise made her stir slightly.

"Good-by, Steve," she said distantly. "Maybe if you hadn't met Sara—"

I turned and walked away, knowing what she was going to say and not wanting to hear it. The door opened silently and I was outside. I shut the door carefully. For the last time.

By the time I'd driven the Olds into the apartment garage I was close to sleep. But at three in the morning Kellaway woke me and we went over it in detail, all of it, and he agreed to keep the emerald out of the papers. After a transfusion Cadena had repeated his confession, which directly implicated Sewall and Bodine, before a police stenographer and witnesses, and a Virginia highway patrol had stopped Cokey Joe just before he reached Southwell. He had neglected to get rid of his gun. The fable about who shot Cadena and why would hang together.

We had a couple of morose drinks, Kellaway and I, and about four o'clock he went away. It took me another two drinks to get back to sleep and when I woke up it was noon and I said the hell with it, and began drinking in earnest.

✤ ✤ ✤

What I got out of it was a small package delivered to my office by a uniformed guard. It was wrapped in silk and sealed with red wax impressed with an Embassy seal. It was the doublet Max Weiskold had made. Half emerald, half fraud, but a beautiful thing. And worth all of twenty thousand dollars.

I keep it in my safe-deposit box at the bank. Every month or so I take it out and fondle it but then I get to remembering how it came to me and so I wrap it up again and put it away. I keep telling myself I ought to sell it and get myself something solid and sensible like a house. Somehow, though, I doubt that I ever will.

Made in the USA
Middletown, DE
26 October 2021

51102696R00111